MARCUS

A MONEY, POWER & SEX NOVELLA

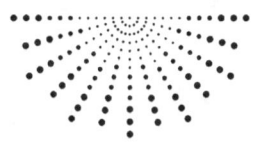

NORIAN LOVE

To Dad
Semper Fi

ACKNOWLEDGMENTS

So I had this idea one day to see what it would be like for a person who loves to read to binge read a series of books, sort of like how you would binge watch a show on Netflix. Thus, Love Season was born.

Over the next few weeks, I wanted to expand on some of the events that happened post-Seduction. When you take on something like this there are a lot of people that are pulling for you behind the scenes and I would be remiss if I didn't thank them.

Starting with my admin for her diligence in helping this concept come together and keeping me on task and away from the shiny new stories. I want to thank everyone who worked on the visuals. There are too many people to single out but just know I value your contributions. I do want to thank Mr. Kae Lavo for his gift and lastly and most importantly I want to thank my family and friends for your support and encouragement.

However, none of this would actually be possible without you, the reader. From the bottom of my heart I truly appreciate your trust that I'm going to give you a story that will entertain you. I hope that in this book, this love season experience is no exception. You'll never know what you mean to me and if we never cross paths in this life, it's important to me that you know I thank you for choosing to spend your time with me. I hope you enjoy it.

WOUNDED WARRIOR

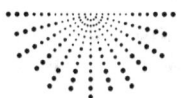

This is not how I will die, he thought to himself. *This is bullshit. After serving my country, saving all those lives, I will not die in the hallway of this house...*

"Help! Somebody help me!"

Marcus forced out a cry. He wasn't sure if it was the bat between his legs or the blow across his back, but he was having one of the most brutal seizures since his diagnosis. And it all happened because he'd tried to make amends with the woman he loved.

"Help!" he yelped again, as forcefully as he could, still to no avail.

He glanced toward the open door and could see her car driving off. There was no one coming to save him, and he was having a hard time breathing.

Maybe the doctor was wrong.

Maybe he didn't have more time than he thought. This was it. He was about to die.

With as much energy as he could muster, he stretched to reach the dresser and pull on the white linen runner that was covering the nightstand. His phone was there, but his erratic hand movements knocked everything off the dresser.

A shard of glass from a now-broken vase lodged in his shoulder.

He was definitely dying. He couldn't control his muscle spasms and motor functions, but somewhere in the recesses of his mind he registered footsteps echoing in the house.

He tried shuffling around to see who it was, but his body wouldn't respond. Abruptly, he felt himself being hoisted upward. Immediately his breathing went back to normal, his muscles relaxed, and he was slowly regaining control of his body.

Through his blurry vision he could see the vague shape of a woman and assumed that Kendra had come back for him. She'd heard him and come back to help him and, with any luck, if he survived, maybe they had a chance to save their relationship. The blossoming hope calmed him, but as his vision cleared, he realized it was Elaine.

"Marcus, breathe! Just breathe."

He felt the strength return to his body. He attempted to support his own body weight, but he wasn't quite there.

"I'm gonna help you to the couch. Use whatever you need to get up and sit down on the sofa, okay? On three. One, two, three."

Marcus used every ounce of strength he had left to stand with Elaine's help. He was physically drained. His muscles had never been this sore in his life. He stumbled onto the couch, the glass shard in his shoulder shooting pain through him.

"I'm gonna get this shard out of you, okay? Just sit tight."

He was bleeding, and it didn't look good. Blood had pooled where he had laid on the floor. Marcus wasn't sure how much he'd lost, and he was starting to panic.

Elaine came back with his first aid kit and could see the alarm in his eyes.

"Hey, hey, Marcus, listen to me. You'll be okay. We're gonna get this out of here and you'll be all right. Now bite this towel."

As he bit down, she slowly removed the glass. The pain intensified as the blood continued running. She helped to remove his shirt and quickly started to dress the wound using the first aid kit.

"All done. Nod if you can understand what I'm saying." Elaine went into her military medical training mode. She was better than he remembered.

He nodded in response.

"I'm going to call 9-1-1 so we can get you to the hos—"

"I'm fine." Marcus interrupted. He could feel his strength return-ing. Elaine smiled with a sigh of relief as she put her hands on either side of his face.

"You didn't look fine right now. Are you sure?"

"I'm fine," he repeated, as he moved her hands from his face. He stood up with little struggle, though his shoulder still throbbed.

Marcus stood up and walked to the kitchen, opening a cabinet and grabbing a bottle of Jack Daniels. He took a swig as he looked Elaine Holt up and down.

"Elaine, I just have one question."

"What's that?"

He lifted his hand to reveal the gun he'd stashed in the cabinet and aimed it at Elaine's face.

"Just what in the hell are you doing here?"

2

THE SOLDIER

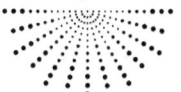

"*M*arcus, I told you I ca—"

"Cut the shit, Elaine. Tell me the truth or I'm pulling this trigger. Let's start with why you're here and what was with all that fucked up shit in your apartment."

"You saved my life, okay!" she screamed, the frustration in her voice reverberating through the hallways of the home.

"What are you talking about?" he asked.

Elaine folded her arms defensively and drawled, "You saved my life, back when we were stationed overseas. I haven't been able to…"

Marcus watched as her eyes shifted downward, as if to recall a memory. She took a deep breath and wiped the tear that was forming. He recognized the look of a debt-ridden soldier. He sat the gun to the side and handed her the bottle. She took a swig and handed it back.

"What are you talking about, when you say I saved your life, Elaine?"

She wiped another tear from her eye, heaved a deep sigh and said. "When I joined the military, I had no fucking clue what I was getting into. I just wanted to pay for college, y'know? The war was dying down – at least that's what I thought at the time. There wouldn't be a need for new soldiers to go over there."

She reached for the bottle and took another sip before continuing. "I'll never forget my recruiter's name. Wayne Skaife. That asshole promised me the world. I can still hear him now. 'Just take the interpreter classes and you're on easy street.' He told me they'd have me translate stuff over walkie talkies, and that a whole new wave of technology was coming. I'd do my entire job from a desk somewhere far from the action. And I believed him because why would he lie about something like that?"

"Recruiters will say anything to get you in," Marcus chimed in as he handed her the bottle again.

Elaine nodded and took another swig from the bottle.

"I wasn't three weeks out of boot camp when we got called up. Afghanistan, of all places, right in the middle of the goddamn action. I remember laughing to myself on the helicopter, because I'd told Skaife what I really wanted was to be as close to home as possible, and not once did he say that I should think about being a recruiter. Damn, I was so green then. I'd never even killed a bug, hadn't gone on an actual date, and then out of nowhere I was surrounded by death and murder. I thought God was punishing me, because it seemed like the more I wished to go home, the worse the assignments got."

This time she didn't bother holding back the tears. They flowed freely as she continued to talk. Marcus softened his stance as she continued.

"One day, Charlie company gets sent out into the field to find an Al-Qaeda defector. He'd promised he could guide us through the region, and they needed an interpreter to figure out if we could trust him and what he was saying in real time."

"And with you being able to speak Arabic plus your background in psychology, you were the perfect candidate," Marcus surmised, putting the pieces together.

She nodded and wiped the tears as she continued. "Now, as I told you, I'm scared shitless. This is my first combat engagement and my sergeant at the time is riding my ass to see if we could trust this guy. I'm panicking, you know?"

"You hesitated," Marcus said.

Elaine nodded and straightened her back. Marcus could tell she was trying to be strong, but he also knew how deep a soldier's unresolved wounds could run.

"I did. I thought I... my training... I..." She trailed off, stuck in her memories, before shaking herself and continuing.

"By time I figured out he was lying, it was too late. A sniper took out my Sarge. We were getting to cover when an RPG took out our number two. Our platoon leader was quickly taken down by a sniper while trying to get the rest of us to cover. After they killed him, I was the highest ranking officer still breathing. That left me in charge. I ordered everyone who'd survived the first wave into an abandoned building, which was a mistake because it was a goddamn kill-box.

"We fought like hell and held up throughout the night, trying to make sure we didn't all die, but they were one step ahead of us. They were picking off the men one by one until I realized they wanted the women alive. I'm sure you can only imagine what that meant. How we survived as long as we did, I'll never know."

Marcus handed her the bottle of liquor again. Elaine took a sip and closed her eyes. He watched as the tears fell onto the counter. She continued.

"That's when Bravo company came riding into the rescue with you leading the charge. You guys fought like the soldiers you see in the movies, and when you found us... when you found me... I had pissed myself because I was so afraid of dying, and you understood. Without a word, you gave me your jacket to cover up, and we got the hell out of there. It was the first time I ever felt safe in the Army."

"I remember that day," Marcus interjected as he reclaimed the bottle for himself. "I held onto your shoulders, and you killed everything that wasn't wearing green, and I thought to myself *it's over, we're gonna make it*, but then a grenade fell next to us."

"Right, we were trying to get the wounded first, but we knew another wave was coming, so we were just putting everyone on the chopper as fast as possible.

"When the grenade fell, you pushed us out of the way right before it went off, but the explosion separated us. When I came to my senses, there was an enemy combatant standing on top of me with his rifle pointed at me. He pulled the trigger, but the gun jammed. That was all you needed to take him out. His body fell on top of me. I soiled myself again, and I thought, *this is it. I'm going to die because he's going to forget about me, and they'll find me and kill me.* But you were there again. You moved his body to pick me up, tossed me over your shoulder and sprinted to the chopper, and before I could process what was happening, we were in the air. I looked at you and you said—"

"'No man left behind.'"

"And you meant it. I've been on deployments where guys would just accept the losses. But you didn't leave me. It was the second time you'd saved my life in one day."

"I was doing my job."

"When we got back to base, I went to medical and, as I was getting patched up, the captain came in and told me I'm getting the medal of valor under the recommendation of Sergeant Marcus Winters.

"Me, the coward just trying to find the best place to hide, was getting a medal because I didn't get killed. While you were deployed again. That night, you saved my life twice and *I* was being rewarded for it. I didn't know how to feel. But I knew one thing for certain: if I had to stay in the military, I knew who I wanted to be like.

"I transferred to Bravo company immediately, and you didn't disappoint. Because under your leadership, you gave me a gift I could never repay. You taught me to save my own life, and I've never been scared again. So, forgive me if I sound crazy, but I love you for that and I'll do anything to prove it to you."

Marcus put the gun back in its drawer.

It was nice to have someone compliment him. Hell, it felt good just to feel good. Marcus knew he was dying, but he also knew he didn't want to dwell on it. He didn't have time to.

He looked at the flowers he'd bought with his last few dollars, a peace offering to an honest realization, and felt foolish. It perfectly summed up his life: a beautiful disaster. This wasn't how it was supposed to end.

Elaine reminded him of the time he was the warrior, a born leader who led his battalion into a victory of twenty-six separate combat engagements with zero casualties. A legend in certain military circles. This wasn't how his story was going to end.

His pride was kicking in.

He glanced at the blood creeping through the patchwork on his shoulder. "Thank you for this." He rotated his arm to feel the extent of the wound, to determine how long it would take to heal.

"I'm glad you approve, but..."

"But what?"

"Can you explain why you were lying on the floor?"

Marcus took a shot of whiskey before he responded. "Because I'm dying."

Her reaction startled him. Her face was pained, as if his life mattered to her. After listening to her story, he could understand why.

He watched as she processed the words, and after a moment she finally asked, "What fro—"

"Ah, it doesn't matter. Some incurable shit too complicated to explain."

"Well, maybe if you tell me and let me help, I could—"

"Elaine, when a man hears shit like this... Just let me have a moment, but the point is, it won't end like this. Not for me."

He took another shot of whiskey. Elaine walked over to him and took the bottle, taking another swig. She looked him in his eyes.

"What can I do to help?"

"I don't need your he—"

"Before you dismiss me, please understand. From my point of view, I just found out the man who I owe my life to, the man I love, is dying. Even after everything that we've been through today, the fact remains that Kendra is gone, and I'm right here where I want to be, to help for however long you have left, if you'll let me. So, I'll ask you again, what can I do to help?"

He found a sullen comfort in her words. The harsh reality of his truth, maybe. He wasn't naïve enough to think that a repeat of the episode he'd just had could be handled on his own, and until this week, she'd been the perfect mistress.

I've got a year left. I could use a support system.

He knew she meant what she said. He also knew she was batshit crazy, and he wasn't sure if he wanted to fight that battle.

"I know what you need," Elaine said as she walked over and stood directly in front of him. She got to her knees and pulled down his pants. She looked him in the eyes and opened her mouth. His body betrayed his will as his dick stiffened at the idea that she was about to give him a blowjob. Whether or not he wanted to admit it, it was exactly what he desired, and if he were being truly honest, he wanted it from her.

She quickly slurped the tip of his manhood, making it jump – almost a confirmation of what was about to happen. His defenses were gone. He watched her big blue eyes looking up into his own, eager to make him feel better.

Without hesitation, she deep-throated his dick, the wetness of her saliva breaking down his walls of hurt and frustration and fear. There was no more denying he wanted her, and he wanted what only she was ever willing to do for him: let him have his way with her.

"Oh, shit," he moaned.

She pulled her lips off of his now-throbbing dick and stared as the combination of pre-cum and saliva dripped from the tip. Still on her knees, she looked up and said, "Well, what are you waiting for? Throat-fuck me."

Marcus looked into her eyes as she opened her mouth seductively to accommodate his manhood. He grabbed locks of her fire-red hair and shoved his dick in her mouth with forcefulness, pushing past her gag reflex. He started to slowly slide his dick between her parted lips, enjoying the moisture and the sensation of them wrapped around his dick. Suddenly she pulled back and, with slight agitation, said, "Is that all you got, soldier? I said throat-fuck me!"

Without hesitation, he grabbed her head more forcefully. He shoved his dick into her throat in a mean-spirited way that she enjoyed.

She moaned, and fought the urge to gag with pleasure as his hard dick hit the back of her throat. She grabbed ahold of his legs to assist in the blowjob's rhythm. She wanted all he could give her.

"Damn baby, this feels so good," he moaned as she said nothing, but continued to allow him to please himself with her mouth. His tension was melting away. At this moment, Kendra and his condition were of no consequence. He was building to a climax. This was exactly what he needed.

"What are you?" he barked as he pulled his dick out of her mouth as he was nearing orgasm.

She looked up and, without hesitation, said, "I'm a cum slut."

Her words excited him as he shoved his dick into the back of her throat. She used her tongue to lick his balls each time he buried his rock-hard dick into her throat. He face-fucked her, feeling nothing but sheer ecstasy.

"Holy shit!" he growled as his cum erupted violently into her throat. "Oh my God!" he yelled as she savagely slurped it into the back of her throat, moaning in enjoyment.

Marcus collapsed onto the ground, this time in pleasure. As he struggled to control his breathing, he had to admit it was the best he'd felt all day.

He glanced at her. *I know she's a bit off, but damn, that shit feels good. She gives head like she made it up.*

He looked into her eyes and was met with a look of satisfaction. He was crazy for even entertaining the idea. He knew it would be a mistake, but it was one he accepted.

She was right. If he were truly honest in this moment, it was exactly what he'd needed. He knew he wanted to keep feeling this way for whatever time left he had on this earth.

She crawled to rest on his chest gingerly, as if asking for unspoken permission. He granted it by extending his arm for her to nestle between his chest and his shoulder. He watched her deep blue eyes look at him with a cool, steel intensity.

"I will always be here for you if you let me, Marcus. You saved my life. I'm just asking you to let me make yours as comfortable as possible."

It was that simple. Her eyes were filled with truth; she meant every word.

"Let me think about it." he said, as the two laid there in the aftermath of chaos.

3
ON THE FRONT LINES

"This fucking red hair again."

The wench sheds like a cat, Marcus thought, cleaning out the bathroom.

It had been weeks since Elaine had moved in. His condition was in flux. There were days he'd feel just like his old self. This was one of those days.

Dr. Packard had gently insisted he take it easy.

That would not happen. He was going out on his terms.

The military instilled in him a need to keep a clean home, and while his new companion was a work in progress, he thoroughly enjoyed cleaning. It provided order and a sense of pride. He often would clean up after Kendra since she was pretty sloppy by his standards, but it was one way he'd found to take a load off while she had been building her career.

"That's the thing about these women: they don't appreciate the small things," he murmured to himself. Marcus was determined not to make that same mistake again.

He walked into the living room and saw Elaine working on one of her client profiles from work. She'd been hovering over him lately, which was annoying, but he had to admit her company wasn't too exhausting.

"Elaine, we need to talk. You're gonna have to clean up after yourself or you gotta go. I'm not gonna spend my last days cleaning up your filth."

"Good morning to you, too. Let me say that, A, I know this has been an adjustment for you, so I'll work on being more mindful. And B, I've never met a man with more OCD than you. You're going to find something to clean no matter what, because in your own words, you've 'got the blood of a janitor but don't want his paycheck'. That's why you joined the Army."

"I'm just saying that I'm not used to having red hair in the sink, or the tub. Hell, anywhere for that matter."

"Marcus, you used to come over to my house and fold my clothes after we had sex. If I knew you were coming over, I'd literally run to throw anything dirty in the washing machine, and then you'd get pissed because I ruined my whites, and you'd just do it yourself. We should discuss what this is really about."

"And what is that?"

"You're feeling despondent and detached since Kendra lived here, and you see me as the catalyst for your previous relationship suffering, and so the red hair is a trigger."

She was right, and he hated it. He squinted his eyes as he replied. "Don't do that."

"You're gonna have to be more specific. What exactly don't you want me to d—"

"That psychobabble shit. It's annoying as hell."

"Okay, how else do you want me to communicate with you? Because every time I give you the truth, your feelings get hurt and you want to run off."

"What? You really are crazy. I have no problem with the truth."

"You see how that was hurtful? I know you need someone to blame, so I'll let that pass."

"Don't tell me what I need. If you have something to say, say it."

Elaine crossed her legs as she closed her book and removed her glasses. She looked at him and said, "Okay, fine. You're the one who asked me to stay over. To basically be your whore, therapist, and punching bag. I haven't said a word because I'm trying to show you how much I care, but now you're mad because my hair is red, even though you've always loved redheads. I'm trying my best to take care of you, Marcus, but I can't change how I was born. So, you gotta ask yourself, are you pissed about my red hair because you still feel this is Kendra's home? Because if so, there's nothing I can do about that. I'll never be Kendra, and I'm not gonna be your emotional punching bag."

The truth was indeed hurtful.

He said nothing, angry with her honesty.

"Look, I know you're dealing with a lot all at once, so I'll take some shit, Marcus. I just don't want you to get used to throwing it my way. I'm here trying to help you."

She was right about all of it. He wanted to admit it to himself. She knew what she was signing up for. He didn't have to love Elaine, he just didn't have to treat her like crap. He had to deal with his anger.

He couldn't be there, not right now. Clearing his mind with a light jog was exactly what he needed. He went to the bedroom and changed into a pair of gym shorts and a lightweight t-shirt.

"I'm going for a jog."

"Marcus, do you think that's a go— "

"I'm going for a jog."

Elaine lifted her hand to stop him and walked over to the hallway closet, taking out a pair of running shoes. He realized she was already wearing leggings and a sports bra. He had an uninvited guest on his trip.

"Elaine, you're not coming with me."

She ignored him as she tied the second shoe and stretched.

"Elaine, I said—"

"If you want to run Marcus, that's fine, but I won't find you on the side of the road because of your ego. I'm coming with you."

"Look, Elaine, I apprec—"

"This isn't me trying to coddle you, either. Your condition is serious, so we're gonna treat it that way. It's the only way to beat it.

Besides, I need the exercise myself, so we can sit around yappin' about jogging or we can jog. Just know, if we are jogging, I'm Bravo company's mile distance record holder. So, when we show up, we fight."

He wasn't stubborn enough to think that there wasn't a possibility of him having another episode outside, but something deeper had been stimulated inside of him. By evoking the name of their military platoon, his pride had kicked in once again. He was now up for the challenge.

"Okay, Holt, let's do it."

The pair headed out of the home and over to the jogging trail close to his home. When they arrived, he considered the two options: the one mile and the 3.10 mile trail, which was the track people used to train for 5k runs.

He looked over to Elaine, who was already standing in front of the second line. He wasn't sure if he was ready for it, but before he could open his mouth, Elaine preemptively said, "No pussy shit, Winters. Let's go, Bravo."

Marcus relented. She was right that he needed to push himself for as long as he could. He walked to the entrance to the trail and began to jog.

He wondered if he would have another episode as they began their journey. Maybe not today, but when? In his sleep, or perhaps while he was driving? As the thoughts began to consume him, he felt a slap on his behind. *Pop!*

"What the he—"

"Bravo doesn't lead from the rear! Now, move your ass!" Elaine shouted as she pulled past him.

She set a pace that made it hard for him to keep up. By the time they were in the second mile, he'd pushed himself to hold the pace. He felt amazing..

All he could focus on was running, and controlling this breathing, and it felt wonderful. He could see the end of the trail after a while. He was relieved.

"Double time to the house, soldier!" Elaine barked as she sprinted past him.

Marcus took this as a challenge and picked up his own pace. She turned back and said, "Is that all you got?"

She picked up her pace again, leaving him behind.

"Oh, hell no," he mumbled as he started to sprint.

He was gaining on Elaine fast, and he could sense when she felt his presence. She ran harder still, but it was no use. He sped past her with ease as he entered the driveway of his home, turned around and taunted her, imitating Rocky.

"Who's the champ?! You thought you could outsprint me? Baby, I own the B company 200 meter record till this day!" he exclaimed with a bravado he relished. He was out of breath, but still felt incredible.

"I let... you beat me," she huffed, still regaining her breath, smiling through the pain of the sprint.

"Yeah, right. You couldn't hang on, and we both know it."

"Whatever, I let up at the end."

He looked at her, and without thinking, he kissed her.

Her body relented at his strength as he pressed her against the wall. Without thought, he pulled his dick out and pulled down her blue spandex pants and slid himself into her already-wet pussy.

They were outside, and it was almost dark, but he was fucking her against the side of the house. She wasn't embarrassed. She was excited as he felt the moisture of her pussy saturate his dick.

"Oh, my god, you're gonna make me cum on your dick," she whispered.

Her nastiness only turned him on more. She gave him full control. He was a man, and with each stroke, there was a beautiful woman submitting herself to him for pleasure, willing to take all he could give in this moment.

He thrust his wood deeper into her pussy with authoritative strokes as her moans of pleasure sounded like muffled yelps as he penetrated her to the point of climax.

"Oh, god!" she screamed out.

He knew his neighbors heard that one, but he didn't care. If they came outside, they would see him fucking a beautiful woman, and what was better than that?

He was alive, doing what he wanted to do in this moment, and that was all the satisfaction he needed. Getting what he wanted, when he wanted it, and Elaine was always more than willing to give it to him without resistance.

This thought pushed him to reach his own climax. He warmed the walls of her pussy with his load, spilling out of her onto the grass.

They both fell limp, exhausted by the animistic nature of their passion.

Marcus looked into the night sky. For the first time since Kendra had left, he felt calm. He wasn't worried about this diagnosis; he wasn't even worried about Kendra.

He looked over at the woman he had to thank for it. The woman who didn't leave him on the ground, who felt she owed her life to him. She was beautiful.

"I'm sorry about earlier. I was tripping."

"You just needed to release some tension. I'm here for you. I want to bring you peace, Marcus. It's all I ever wanted."

He looked into her eyes. He'd spent years interrogating enemy combatants and had watched countless films on human micro-expressions. She wasn't lying. Not at this moment.

What would she have to gain?

He was dying, and she knew it, and she was still there. If she wanted to kill him, he'd have been dead long before now. She wanted to honor the man she fell in love with. Marcus Winters. A beacon to the man he longed to be again.

"Thank you," Marcus said, endearingly kissing her on her forehead as he rubbed her shoulder.

"Oh, babe, I should be thanking you. Your dick is—"

"Thank you for believing in me."

Elaine gingerly looked into his eyes. She extended her hand in their old Army mantra. "Bravo never quits, Bravo never fails."

"Bravo fights," he finished. For the first time since Kendra had left, he was at peace. Yet, the more he thought about it, the more he realized this was the first time he was at peace since before Kendra had left. In fact, the only times he could remember being at peace were with Elaine.

Why am I fighting this?

It was a bad idea, after all. Elaine was certifiably crazy, but maybe it didn't matter. However long his days may be, she was willing to provide companionship, comfort, and good sex. Did anything else matter at this point?

"What are you thinking about?" Her voice interrupted his thought.

"Honestly... you. I was thinking about you."

4
HOOAH!

"*J*ust two more, Winters," Ryan Hayes, Marcus' old war buddy, barked as Marcus pushed the weight into the air.

Though he felt strong, he knew at any moment his legs, arms, or entire body could give out, so he'd been working with a much lighter weight than he could normally press. His plan was working fine until Hayes called him out on being soft, and his ego took over. He was now squatting his max weight, regretting it with each thrust.

"One more, Winters, goddamn it! Push!"

His mind focused on the weight, but he could feel the fatigue in his legs settling in like foam crème on a Frappuccino. Every part of him wanted to give up. He glanced at Hayes, who recognized the unspoken moment all too well and gave him exactly what he needed.

"You son of a bitch, if you don't move those goddamn legs, I'm gonna kick your ass and bang your sister in that order!"

It was all the motivation he needed. Marcus pushed with all of his might to get the machine back in a proper position.

"That's thirteen," he barked. He stood up precariously, sore all over, and loved it.

"Nice work there, Winters. For a second there I was wondering if I was here with a man and not some candy-ass toddler afraid of a little hard work, but your nuts finally dropped."

"Thanks, Hayes. Also, fuck you, Hayes. Even sick, I'm kicking your ass."

"You got a point there. Hell, between this and the four miles we just ran, I'd think you're playing possum."

"Or maybe I'm just a bad motherfucker. Bravo never quits."

"If I gotta hear that shit one more time, you won't have to wait for the disease to take you out. I'll shoot you myself."

The pair chuckled as Ryan racked the weights while Marcus looked around the VA's workout facility. He loved it there and was slowly realizing he always would. The camaraderie between soldiers was something you couldn't explain, you just had to experience. They understood him and he them. Everything had an order, even dying.

Not to mention it was the best place for him to get his mind off Kendra. Even though Elaine had all but moved in, he still missed KD. He thought about her every day; he'd been working extra hard lately to stay away from her social media, and so far was succeeding. Last time he'd looked, he'd seen images of her new man, Desmond, who he'd taken to calling *that motherfucker Desmond*. The guy she'd met on the islands.

Marcus wasn't over her, and he wasn't happy that she could move on so quickly, yet he knew he sounded like a hypocrite. He was with Elaine, and she was bringing balance to his life in a way he really needed, but also appreciated.

In a nutshell, life was good. Elaine provided all the food, sex, and comfort he could handle. Still, even with her catering to his every desire, he wasn't in love with her. Not the way he loved Kendra. He missed the sound of her voice and he missed making love to her. He missed feeling her love.

Buzz.

He pulled out his phone and looked at the incoming message, partly hoping it was Kendra. But he knew exactly who it was.

Did you kick his ass today?

Bravo never fails.

When you get home, I'm giving you the 3 Bs. Breakfast, blowjob, back rub, you choose the order.

He was grinning at her response when Hayes started yelling in his right ear.

"Goddamn it, Winters, are we working out, or are you gonna finger-bang that nutjob Holt with your phone all day?"

"Elaine isn't a nut, Hayes. Watch yourself," he said instinctively.

The comment made Ryan's eyebrows raise as high as he'd ever seen them. "Holy shit. As I live and breathe. You're falling for Holt, aren't you?"

"What? I... no, it's just... she gets a bad rap, that's all."

"Don't lie, Winters, you aren't good at it."

Marcus took a sip of the water bottle. *Why am I denying her?*

He looked to Ryan, who was smiling like a kid getting ice cream for dessert. He knew he had to respond.

"I mean, she's growing on me, that's for sure."

Ryan clapped his hands together and smirked. "Well, congratulations."

Marcus could sense the twinge of sarcasm in his tone.

Ryan adjusted the pectoral fly machine and lifted the weight.

"You mean that, Hayes?"

"I most certainly do. I learned a long time ago to stay out of a man's way when he's about to make a dumb decision. You play stupid games, you win stupid prizes... so congratulations."

Marcus was slightly offended by his comrade's response, but his words resonated with feelings he had in the back of his mind. He wanted clarity, no matter how harsh it was going to be.

"And what's that supposed to mean?"

Hayes stopped his workout and looked at Marcus sincerely. "Look, you're a smart guy. If we're going into battle, or a bar fight, there's no one in the world I'd rather have by my side, 'cept maybe Chavez. But with women, you're as dumb as a bag of dicks. The woman has more than a few screws loose, and if you keep getting your dick wet there, let's just say you're in for a hell of a ride."

There was a sinister truth to what Ryan said. The kind of truth he'd buried, considering the little time he had left.

Ryan finished his set and allowed Marcus to get on the machine.

"You know, maybe dying is doing something to my memory, 'cause I don't recall you being the type of guy to say something like that without facts."

Marcus got up from the machine and drank the water Ryan handed him.

Ryan looked around and stepped closer. "Let me fill you in on something. Remember when those assholes wanted to show the world that the military was having fun while killing baddies, and they got the bright idea of having a mock Olympic games? What was it called?"

"The General's games, right? They sent us a form, and we were supposed to select a male and female soldier at random."

"Yeah, that bullshit. Now this was back when I didn't know who you were, but everyone treated you like black Jesus with a 9 mm, and I hated everything about Bravo Company. From your stupid mantra to your stupid faces. I just wanted to kick your asses, so to make sure that our 'random selection' was only our very best, we had an internal competition."

"Wait, are you telling me you rigged your side?"

"You're damn right I did."

"But how—"

"It's best not to dwell on the past. The point is, we sent C company's best to represent us in the qualifier. Holt was in my battalion at the time. She wanted to prove herself so bad. I had it in my mind I wasn't gonna select her, though, because we had some studs. Now, she was always good at PT and, truth be told, she was supposed to be a favorite to win all the PT events. She was about as good as they come on the gun range, but the obstacle course was gonna do her in. It was pretty common knowledge in the barracks that Parker owned the swimming pool, and Carter was our best distance runner; she was never gonna beat them. Her best times were putting her in about third place, so all those other two had to do was hang in and then take their chances on the obstacle course."

"Where is this going, Ryan?"

"Cool your jets, Maverick, I'm gettin' there. So, three days before, everyone was just dog-tired. I could see it in their eyes, but I didn't give a shit. I wanted to win. Then Holt comes to me and, in a very subtle way, points out I've been riding everyone pretty hard and they could use a bit of R&R before the big event. At first, I was against it, but she's the shrink, so I think this might not be such a bad idea, so screw it. Everyone goes out to drink, including Holt. They had a pretty good time too, nothing they couldn't sweat or sleep off the next day. So, I wasn't worried about them showing up their best."

Ryan started to adjust the weight machine and sat down to use it as he continued.

"Thing is, the next morning both Carter and Parker had the shits. I mean, they looked miserable. I sent them to the doc; they somehow contracted a stomach bug that would keep them out of commission for the next few days. But Holt was just fine."

Marcus shrugged his shoulders, indifferent to the story he was hearing. "Yeah, that's a weak argument. There's a thousand reasons for that. Do you think Holt was just walking around with a stomach bug in her pocket? Maybe they were lightweights."

"You ever met a lightweight drinker in the military, Winters? I've seen Parker drink a pint of tequila like it was rose water before running ten miles."

Marcus nodded in agreement of his comrade's assessment. "Okay, Hayes, so what's your point?"

"My point is, pull your head out of her snatch and smell the shit, Winters. Something stinks with that one, always has. No matter what happens, she always seems to come out on top, and there's always collateral damage."

Marcus processed his words. He was about to respond when he glanced across the VA and saw someone he thought he recognized.

"Hold that thought."

He looked closer. Something was definitely familiar about the woman.

He stepped toward her, hoping to conceal his gaze, but it was too late. His staring, while confirming his suspicions, also garnered the attention of the stranger he was trying to examine. His eyes met her smile.

"I'll be damned, Shanice Gibson!" he said aloud.

She started toward him, and he met her halfway, greeting her with a giant bear hug. He could smell the lavender and vanilla-scented lotion that moisturized her almond-brown skin as she squeezed him tightly, chuckling with excitement.

After a long hug, Marcus said, "Corporal Gib—"

"Ah, ah...Check the stripes. It's Sergeant First Class now. "

"Well! My mistake, *Sergeant First Class* Gibson."

"I'm getting used to correcting people. It's good to see you, Marcus."

"It's good to see you too, Gib. The stripes look good on you."

Shanice smiled and nodded. "Thanks. I've wanted them since I first saw you with them."

"Oh, I remember how jealous you were of me," he joked.

Gibson punched him in the arm and responded. "Whatever, Marcus. I'm actually surprised to see you. I thought you'd moved to Houston?"

"I did for a sec, but I moved back home a while ago. I just missed military life. No place like home, right?"

Shanice nodded in agreement. "I can relate to that. It's the reason I'm back."

Marcus glanced at her ring finger. The engagement ring she used to wear was nowhere to be found.

"Don't tell me Darius cheated," he said confidently.

Her eyes revealed he was right.

"Same old Winters. Goddamn know-it-all."

He laughed out loud. Darius was a ladies man. Marcus had warned her about his behavior during their days in the Army. It was a recurring conversation.

"I hate to tell you I told you so but— "

"Then don't. I can't afford the therapy. Besides, we can't all get a Marcus."

"What's that supposed to mean?"

"It means it's no secret Kendra was always a lucky woman. No need to rub it in our faces."

Marcus chuckled nervously at her response.

It wasn't the fact that he and Kendra were no longer together; it was the stark contrast of the man Shanice remembered, and who he was today. A two-time cheat who was fighting to put together a decent life with what little time he had left.

"*Was* a lucky woman. I'm not with Kendra anymore. And I was the lucky one."

"Oh really? I gotta admit, I didn't see that one coming. But I get it. Relationships are hard. So, who's the flavor of the month?"

"I am," a voice interrupted. Elaine had appeared behind him.

Marcus watched Shanice's face as surprise took over.

She struggled to find her words. "Oh! You and... Holt."

"Uh... yeah, I'm kicking it with Elaine. We, um—"

"We're not labeling anything," Elaine interjected. "Marcus, honey, we need to be leaving. You don't want to be late for your appointment. So nice to see you, Gibson. Take care of yourself."

It was now Marcus who struggled to find his words. He stood silently in the awkwardness created by Elaine's unexpected presence.

Shanice glanced at him and then back at Elaine. "Right... nice to see you, too, Holt. Both of you. Um, take care Marcus."

Stunned, he said nothing as Shanice walked further into the gym.

"Babe, you ready?"

He walked with her in silence. He was trying to hide his frustration, but the longer he walked, his simmer became a boil. By the time they got outside, his frustration was boiling over.

He turned to Elaine and blurted, "What the hell was that?"

"What?"

"Why did you have to—"

"What? Interrupt the shit-eating-grin competition between you and Gibson? Because if you recall, I wanted to make you breakfast, massage those muscles and suck your dick until I taste you. But I also have a job I need to get to. What is she doing back here anyway? I thought she lived in… someplace else."

"Not sure. I said hello to her, and the next thing I knew, you were there," Marcus said, frustrated by her question and general presence.

Elaine turned red, and he realized Hayes was standing near the window, swirling his finger at the side of his head to show he was dealing with a crazy person. That bothered him even more.

He turned back to Elaine and kissed her unexpectedly. Her blush replaced the anger on her face.

"What was that for?"

"To erase any doubts you may have about us. I'm sorry."

He turned to the window to find Hayes shaking his head as he turned around.

Hayes doesn't know shit.

"Marcus," Elaine interjected

"Yeah, babe?"

"I was saying, let's get out of here. Your three Bs await."

The pair had just turned to the car when Marcus heard the noise.

Pop, pop.

The echoes of gunshots not far away.

5
UNDER FIRE

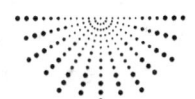

*I*nstinctively, Marcus and Elaine dove to the ground. Adrenaline surged through his veins as he tried to make sense of what was happening.

He scanned the area. Military police were running towards a nearby building.

"That's the rec center," Elaine said, as they continued to assess the situation.

Pop, pop.

"Sounds like a .45 caliber," he said. "We gotta make it inside the gym."

Elaine nodded in agreement.

"Let's move," Marcus said.

The pair got off the ground and, still crouching, ran towards the entrance of the VA gym. As soon as they were inside, they ran into Hayes and Gibson, who were trying to figure out what was happening.

Hayes looked at Marcus. "What in the hell is going on?" he demanded.

"Not a clue. But the gunshots came from the rec center."

Marcus looked out the window. Several soldiers were running away as the military police set up a perimeter around the building.

"Okay, I just got a message. One shooter. It's Jackson," Gibson said to the group.

"Darrell Jackson?" Marcus asked.

"Sounds like it."

"His wife just left him. He hasn't been well. I haven't been able to get through to him at all," Elaine chimed in.

Marcus took inventory of the situation. He looked at the group. "Okay, Jackson is one of ours. Served with B and C companies. If we don't get him to stand down, the MPs are gonna do it and it's gonna be ugly."

"So, what's the play?" Hayes asked.

Marcus peered out the window and looked back at the group. "We're going in. Hayes, you were his last commanding officer, so you, me and Gib are gonna try to talk him down. Holt, you treated him, so see if you can leverage that to get the MPs to give us some time."

"Marcus, I'm his therapist. Shouldn't I go in and Gibson try to talk to the MPs?"

Gibson balked at that. "Holt, he fought side by side with everyone except you. So quit being a bit—"

"Goddamn it, we don't have time for this!" Marcus interrupted. "Look, I know you two aren't best friends, but honestly, I don't give a shit. In fact, nothing else matters except this soldier's life. Are we clear?"

The two were silent.

"I said, are we clear?"

"We're clear," Elaine repeated.

"We're good," Gibson chimed in.

"What do you need us to do?" Hayes asked.

"We're gonna make our way to the entrance. You two are with me. Holt, you're on the MPs. If they deny us, we don't stop until we lay eyes on Jackson. Everyone clear on what we need to do?" He waited for everybody to nod. "Let's move."

The quartet made their way to the perimeter of the blockade.

Holt moved to talk to the officer in charge of the military police. After a spell, she returned.

"Well, he's pissed, but you got five minutes, and then shit gets biblical," she said.

Marcus nodded in agreement. "Alright guys, on my six, let's move."

Before they could leave, Elaine grabbed Marcus by the arm. "Marcus, be careful."

He nodded in understanding as the trio went in. Holt went back over to the blockade.

As they entered the building, Marcus noticed bullet holes in the flat screen television and in the walls.

"No bodies. Doesn't look like he's trying to hurt anyone," Gibson said.

"That could change at any second. Keep your eyes open," Marcus ordered.

As they scanned the area, they spotted broken glass and wood fragments on the ground. Several shots had taken out most of the lighting, which was flickering in and out.

"Winters, over here."

Marcus looked in the direction Hayes was beckoning. Corporal Jackson had barricaded himself against the wall, using furniture in the room.

Marcus lifted his hand to instruct the others to proceed with caution.

As they neared the room, Marcus called out. "Is that a Bravo company fighting man I see?"

"Shit no, Winters, that's a Charlie company soldier," Hayes chimed in.

"Winters? Hayes? Is that you?"

"You know it, Jackson."

"Holy shit. I never thought I'd see the day you two would be doing anything together 'cept fighting."

"Well, when it's important enough, even hard asses like these two can come together, and you're important enough," Gibson chimed in.

"Who is that? Is that Gibson?" Jackson asked.

"That's Gib, she's here with us, checking in on you. We're gonna come inside the room now. We just want to talk, okay?"

There was silence as they walked into the room.

They found the five-foot-ten, brown-skinned man in the corner with a pistol pointed at his head. He was panting and sweating profusely.

Marcus held his hands in the air to show he was unarmed. Hayes and Gibson did the same as they carefully approached.

After a few paces, Jackson pointed the gun in their direction. "That's far enough."

"Okay, okay. We're just here for a little support, Jackson. Hear you've been having a rough go of it."

"My life is over, Sarge. I can't get the shit we've done out of my head. I'm a danger to everyone."

"That's not true. I know because you saved my life a couple of times, Jackson," Gibson chimed in.

"She's right. I was there to see it," Hayes said. "I've been where you've been, brother. Right where you've been. Hell, wasn't but a few months ago they had me in the psych ward because the darkness tried to get a hold of me, but Winters helped me through it. Let us help you now."

Marcus took another step closer. He was too far away to prevent Jackson from killing himself, or the three of them, but he knew he had to get as close as possible.

Marcus looked into the soldier's eyes. He was calming down. They were getting through to him.

Marcus stepped closer and calmly said, "Jackson, you're having a bad day. We've all been there. But you gotta remember, it's just a day. It's not your entire life. *You* define the rest of your life. If we can just get to tomorrow, I promise it's going to be better. I know that for a fact.

"A few months ago, I found out I was dying. You know, most of us military guys, we don't have a rich family history. All we have is each other. We're the only ones who care about each other's feelings. The day I found out I was dying, my woman left me. I had nothing. My first instinct was to do what you're thinking about doing, but here I am talking to you."

He knew his words stunned Gibson and Jackson, surprised by his honesty.

"You're... dying?"

"Yeah, some kind of acute Parkinson's. Doc gave me about a year to live. It's gonna be ugly in the end too. Now, imagine on the day you find out you're dying, your lady hits you in the nuts with a bat. Literally. And while you're on the ground having a seizure, she tells you she's going to go be with a guy she met on a tropical island."

"Holy shit, Winters, that's horrible."

"Yeah, man. I look up after a while, dealin' with all that and all I could think was: does my dick still work?"

Jackson laughed loudly. As the room joined in, Marcus took another step closer. Jackson waved the gun to show he'd come far enough and then gingerly asked, "Ending it all... what stopped you?"

Marcus took another step closer. "For starters, I realized that, while I may not have much family, I made my own. I had nothing else in the world but you guys, and I didn't want to let them down. You have a little girl, right, Jackson?"

"Yeah, Caprice. She's nine."

"Do you have a picture of her?"

Jackson reached into his wallet and tossed it to Marcus, who opened it and saw a picture of his daughter.

"Oh, man, she's beautiful. You're gonna have to be here to protect her from these Army guys. Especially a guy like Hayes. He's a real perv."

Jackson chuckled in response.

Marcus glanced over at Gibson and Hayes, who were both nodding in unspoken agreement.

Keep him talking.

Marcus stepped closer.

"The shit we've seen, man. No one tells you that once you come back stateside, you're enlisted in a different war. The one in your head."

Jackson lowered the gun, still in a defensive position, but Marcus could tell he was getting through to him.

"How did you, all of you, get past all the pain, man?"

Hayes took one step closer casually before saying, "I'm not gonna bullshit you. I drank a lot at first. Then I realized I had family right here. These were my brothers and sisters in arms. Right now, I still struggle, but I'm here for Winters, Gibson, and you. Because you're worth fighting for. I won't leave you behind on the battlefield, brother."

"None of us will," Marcus interjected as he also took a step closer. "I'll make a deal with you. You get through today and we'll all get together and have this talk tomorrow and every day after that. Same time. You have my word, you can trust me. I'll keep fighting my battle just so we can talk. I wanna live, Jackson, and I know you do too. Give me a reason to wake up tomorrow, man. Give me the gun, Jackson. You don't want to do this. Everything else we can work out, man, just give me the gun."

Marcus watched as the soldier's eyes went soft and he slowly extended his hand towards Marcus, who carefully walked closer to retrieve the weapon.

A message blared over the PA system.

"Corporal Jackson, this is Staff Sergeant Revis! You're surrounded. You have till the count of five to come out with your hands up or this isn't gonna end well for you!"

A jolt of fear rushed through Marcus as he heard the words over the loudspeaker.

He looked at Shanice. "Gib! Get those assholes to stand down! Now!"

"On it!"

As Gibson left, Marcus turned back to Jackson, who was no longer calm. His eyes were dilated. His breathing was heavy, and he gripped the pistol tightly again.

"Jackson, don't listen to them. Brother, it's just us."

"I'm sorry, Sarge. Tell my daughter I love her."

"Jackson, listen man, forget those assholes. They don't know what the—"

Before he could finish his sentence, Jackson put the gun against his temple and pulled the trigger.

Pop.

6

ACTION JACKSON

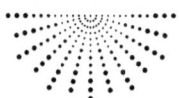

*M*arcus stormed out of the rec center, followed by Gibson and Hayes.

He walked directly up to Staff Sergeant Revis, who had made the announcement.

"You stupid son of a bitch, you killed him!"

"Watch who you're talking to, Winters. You're not in charge of shit but your mouth on this base."

"Then I'll say it. You killed him, you smug son of a bitch!" Hayes yelled as the military police went inside to secure the area.

Revis stayed behind to confront Marcus, Ryan, Shanice, and Elaine.

"I gave you guys five minutes. Time was up. Don't get mad at me because you couldn't get the job done," he said.

Marcus walked closer to him. "Revis, you say one more thing and you're gonna need to make an appointment with the base dentist."

"Cool it, guys!" Elaine chimed in. "Tempers are high right now. Marcus, what happened in there?"

"I talked him down, Elaine. He was just about to hand me the weapon when this asshole gets on the PA system, saying this isn't gonna end well. Which, by the way, is the dumbest thing you could ever say to a guy thinking about taking his own life."

"I did my job! Which is more than I can say for the—"

Before he could finish his sentence, Marcus hit him firmly in the jaw with a devastating right cross. Revis fell to the ground, holding his jaw in pain.

Revis looked at him and pointed to Gibson. "I want this man arrested. Detain him."

"Being the highest ranking officer here, this is my call, and I didn't see anything. Did you, Hayes?"

"I was tying my shoe," Hayes replied.

Marcus hovered over the man and was contemplating hitting him again when Elaine stopped him. "Marcus, calm down! We're all gonna need to be debriefed, so cool off and get out of here. Start heading towards the colonel's office," she said.

Marcus looked at Revis again and then back at Elaine.

"Don't make the situation worse," she pleaded.

He nodded and looked back at Revis. "His blood is on your hands, you prick."

The quartet went to the colonel's office to recall their version of events. After several hours, Marcus, Hayes and Gibson were dismissed, while Elaine had to remain behind, since she was his primary therapist.

The trio off base went to a nearby bar while they waited on Elaine. The Green Mile was named after the famous movie and served as a regular rest stop for soldiers after their shifts.

As the trio walked into the bar, they got a table next to the dartboard, and Marcus ordered three shots of Don Julio 1942.

"Fucking Jackson, man, I can't believe it," Gibson said.

"You two went through basic training together, right?" Hayes asked.

"Yeah, we were close. Did everything together. When we got deployed, he went over to C company to serve under Hayes, and I didn't see him again until my last month overseas when he was deployed to Bravo company."

"We used to call him Action Jackson. Always kept himself busy," Hayes chimed in.

"Definitely the kind of guy you wanted in the foxhole to watch your six," Marcus added as the shots of tequila arrived.

Marcus lifted his shot in the air, followed by Hayes and Gibson.

"To Darrell 'Action' Jackson."

The trio nodded and downed their shots. Marcus ordered another round and recalled the day. Throughout the time he'd been fighting for his own life, he'd never taken into consideration how much the men under his command were fighting for theirs. He was thinking about the day's events and how close he'd come to saving his friend's life.

After a spell, he pounded the table. "Damnit! I almost had him."

"Don't do that to yourself, brother. You had him," Hayes interjected. "That son of a bitch Revis screwed the pooch on this one."

"He's right, this isn't on you, Winters. On any of us. You did everything in your power to save Jackson's life, including sharing your story, which had to be tough to do," Gibson said as she rested her hand on his shoulder comfortingly.

"I appreciate it, guys, but I am responsible. Three years we were in the war zone. I didn't lose a single man. I come back home and I feel like I abandoned everyone."

"That's the job, Marcus," Gibson replied. "You did your duty while we were gone, but it's time for—"

"Not to disagree with you, Shanice, but that isn't the job. It's my job – no it's my duty – to make sure that all of my men and women transition back to stateside well."

"And just how in the hell do you plan on doing that?" Hayes asked.

The words stopped Marcus in his tracks.

"I'm not sure. I was lost when I got back home. Maybe that's why I screwed things up with Kendra. But look, all I know is, as long as I'm alive, I'm not losing another soldier."

The gravity of the words settled around the table.

The trio raised another shot of tequila, as if to cement the pact of the words he'd just uttered. Marcus watched his comrades' energy lift, inspired by his words.

"What's the play, Winters?" Hayes asked.

"Well, from what I can tell, the biggest problem is people not getting enough counseling, and I'm not talking about therapy after you pull a trigger. They need more than the shit the Army provides when they kick you out the door; tools and real-life advice for getting on with life."

"So what are you suggesting, Marcus?" Gibson asked.

"I don't know, Gib, maybe some sort of group session where we talk about how to get our lives back on track, and be able to talk through some of the shit we had to do. Like it or not, once you take up arms and kill someone, we join a different fraternity. Only a few people understand that."

"You're right. We're brothers in arms."

"I like the sound of that, Hayes! Brothers in Arms. That's what it should be called, because once you become a member of this family, it's hard as hell to go back to civilian life. We'll bridge the gap."

"You know, Winters, I always thought you were a stupid son of a bitch, but this idea ain't half bad. I want in," Hayes said.

Marcus laughed. He knew that was the best he'd get from Ryan Hayes. He also knew that once Hayes committed to something, he had his full support.

Another round of shots came and Marcus lifted the glass in the air, followed by the other two.

"To Brothers in Arms."

"Hear, hear!" the trio said as they downed the shots. Shanice dropped her glass and picked it up to make sure it wasn't damaged.

The trio were approached by a man in a Navy uniform. Marcus recognized Melvin Thomas.

"Well, ain't this cute? A bunch of Army rats trying to act like real military men."

The words angered Marcus as he turned around.

"What did you just say?" Hayes asked, standing up to respond to the man who was clearly intoxicated.

37

Melvin responded. "I said the Army wouldn't know its head from its ass."

"Dude, I've had a long day and if you don't sit your ass down—"

"Chill out, Hayes, I got this one," Gibson said.

Marcus glanced over and assessed the situation. He then turned around and orders three beers while Gibson walked and talked to the drunken Navy soldier and his friends. She had this covered.

"You know, Thomas, I don't know if that's your head on your shoulders or your ass, 'cause every time you open your mouth nothing but raw shit falls out."

The crowd laughed as Thomas got upset by the reaction. "Just like Army boys to have a woman deal with their troubles. Look, Gibson, why don't you stay in your place?"

"And where is that?"

"On your knees with your hands around my dick."

The crowd laughed again. Shanice smiled.

"It's cute you think you have enough of a package that I'd need two hands, 'cause word on base is all it would take is a pair of tweezers."

The crowd laughed again as Thomas confronted Gibson.

"Look, bitch, I don't hit ladies, but if you want to act like a man, I'll treat you like one."

Marcus took a sip of his beer. Without glancing at her, he asked, "You good, Gib?"

"Fine like wine, Winters," Gibson said as she continued the conversation. "You know that's funny, Thomas, because your girl told me you had a hard time hitting anything right. In fact, what was the term she used? Oh yeah, 'baby dick'."

The crowd laughed hysterically.

Thomas, clearly wounded by the comment, struck Gibson in the face, sending her stumbling back two steps. Hayes was about to jump up to go after Thomas when Marcus stopped him.

"Hold on, she's got this."

As he continued to sip his beer, he asked again, "You good, Gib?"

"Fine, Winters." She turned her attention back to her assailant. "I guess the rumors about you are true. No matter how hard you try, you really can't make a girl feel anything."

Her words enraged the man, who yelled, "Motherfucker!"

Thomas swung again.

This time, Gibson used her left foot to trip his right leg, forcing him to lose his balance. As he stumbled to the ground, she thrust her left knee forcefully into the air, connecting with the lumbering man's chin, knocking him unconscious immediately.

Before Thomas' two mates could react, she hit one in the throat, then quickly followed up by smashing a glass over his head, rendering him unconscious. The third man charged her, wrapping her in a bear hug.

Hayes was about to get up again when Marcus stopped him a second time. He turned around to watch as Gibson took both of her hands and slammed them into the man's ears, forcing him to release her as he held his head. She then kicked him in his knee, forcefully dislocating it as the man fell. Holding the wounded knee, she elbowed him in the face, knocking him out cold.

"Holy shit, didn't know Rambo had a black sister," Hayes said, impressed by Gibson's fighting ability.

Marcus grabbed him by the shoulder and gleamed with pride as years of training and sparring with Gibson was on display – and was as fierce as he remembered. "This is why your platoon could never beat us in the General's games, Hayes. Because Bravo fucking fights!" he said, patting his friend on the back as Hayes reluctantly nodded in agreement.

The men still laid sprawled out, bleeding. Marcus turned around as five more Navy men stood up and started walking over to Gibson as she backed up.

Marcus finished his beer and stood up.

"You good, Gib?"

"Uh, I could use a little help."

Marcus tapped Hayes on the shoulder. It was their turn to get in on the action.

As the men rushed them, Marcus, Shanice, and Ryan brawled with the well-trained men, beating them convincingly until the military police arrived to break it up.

As they were tossed in the back of the paddy wagon, the trio laughed.

It was like old times; the kind of trouble that could only happen on a military base, and the kind of trouble they'd needed after today's events.

After a spell, Shanice yelled, "That was for you, Jackson!"

7

GOT YOUR SIX

"*H*ow much longer are you guys gonna hold us?" Ryan Hayes asked the guard standing by the holding cell. The MP was silent.

"Ain't this some shit? The one time I could freakin' use some white privilege, this asshole wants to decline me. See, I told you that shit was a myth, Winters."

"I think it's 'cause you're blond, and he has a thing for redheads."

"Or maybe there's a darker reason, or two," Hayes said, making direct eye contact with Gibson and Marcus. They all chuckled at his wit.

Shanice, still laughing, leaned over and said, "Look, I need to get out of here because you aren't gonna have me laughing all night when my damn jaw feels like it's been hit by a bulldozer."

"Now that you mention it, I'm surprised by you, Gib," Marcus interjected.

"What do you mean?"

"I've seen you take harder hits than that on the battlefield, and you never stumbled."

Shanice nodded in agreement with Marcus's words. "I'll admit, being stateside might have made me a little soft, but I still kicked both of your asses tonight."

Marcus stood up in protest. "Wait a minute! What are you talking about? There were five Navy men in there. I took out two and Hayes took out another two. That left you with one."

"True, but I took out the first three by myself, so by my count I took out four to your two apiece."

Marcus was about to protest when Shanice tilted her head to the side, as if to say *would you like to try me?* Both men jokingly raised their hands up to show they wanted no part of it.

"Hey, you'll get no argument from me, She-Ra. The woman kicked both of our asses in an ass-kicking competition. Makes me wonder what you'd be like in the sack," Hayes said, smirking at her.

Shanice walked over to Ryan and sat on his lap, looking seductively into his eyes.

"Ryan Hayes, you are one sexy motherfucker, but you couldn't handle this pussy in your wildest wet dream," she said as she stood up and shoved his forehead playfully.

The trio laughed aloud. Marcus looked at his former second in command and smiled. "Same old Gib. It's good to see you."

"You too, Marcus. It's like old times. Start the day on base, end the night in a holding cell." They continued to laugh until Shanice took a more serious tone. "Look, I know we haven't talked in a while, but why didn't you tell me you were sick?"

"Honestly, Gib, I've just come to grips with it. It's difficult to accept that your days are numbered. Between losing Kendra and getting the diagnosis, I had a lot of shit going on. I'm just now remembering how much this life means to me. How much all of you mean to me."

"Screw that," Ryan Hayes interrupted. "What I want to know is how in the hell did you get hooked up with that nutjob Holt."

Marcus felt a little offended by his friend's statement.

As the pair laughed, Gibson added, "I mean, I didn't want to sound insensitive about the dying thing, but I gotta admit, out of all the things that I've seen and heard today, that shocked me the most."

Marcus nodded, conceding their claim. "Alright, I get it, guys.

Look, I'm here for a good time, not a long time. The way I see it is, she feeds me, fucks me, makes sure I need to be where I need to be. We both know what we've signed up for, and a man shouldn't die alone."

"Can't be with the one you love, so you're loving the one you're with. I get it," Shanice said as she stretched out on the bench.

There was a brief silence, and after a spell, Ryan said, "Yeah, but Holt?"

The trio laughed again. This time, Marcus was a little more defensive in his response. "Hey man, she's actually pretty good to me. Mind your business, Hayes."

"Quiet," the guard ordered, as another guard walked into the room and whispered in his ear. After their exchange, the guard opened the door.

"Winters, it's time to go."

Marcus looked back at his friends, who had all arrived at the same conclusion: Elaine had sprung him and him alone.

"I'll be back for you both," he said.

"Had a great time, Marcus. Let's do it again soon," Gibson said jokingly.

Marcus flipped the two of them off and walked outside. He was relived to be out of the holding cell, but slightly agitated that Elaine didn't post bail to spring them all.

As he walked out of the building, he saw Elaine visibly agitated. He heaved a sigh and walked to hug her. She pushed him away, which he knew meant he had a lot to answer for.

"So, is this what I can expect? You spending time with Gibson?"

"Elaine, I just found out earlier today that she was on base."

"And now you're coming out of a holding cell. For a bar fight, nonetheless."

"Well, what can I say? Bravo fights."

"This isn't funny, and it definitely isn't old times, Marcus. You have to be more careful, especially with your condition. Have you even taken your medication?"

"I'm completely aware of my condition, Elaine. You won't stop reminding me of it. You know what? Despite having a shitty day, I had fun tonight, which is something I can say is a rare occurrence."

"So, are you saying we don't have fun together?"

"That's not what I said," Marcus said as she stormed off.

Marcus caught her by the hand and pulled her in close. Looking into her eyes, he said, "Look, I appreciate you and you know that, but with everything going on, the last thing I need is this raincloud of yours."

Elaine was visibly stunned. "How do you think this makes me feel, Marcus? I'm sitting at home, worried sick about you after what happened, only to find out you're on a date with Gibson."

"It wasn't a date."

"Well, what would you call it?"

"If we're describing the words coming out of your mouth right now, I would call it some bullshit. You know we're all a little wound up after what happened with Jackson, so we grabbed a few drinks. We were waiting for you to join us when some Navy assholes started to—"

"It doesn't matter. You two together have always been trouble. Besides, you shouldn't even be drinking in your condi—"

"Goddamn it, I know what my condition is, Elaine! Just… look, we all needed to blow off some steam. It got out of hand, but Jackson was one of ours, and today hurt. I'm sorry if it hurts your feelings, but honestly, I don't owe you or anyone an explanation for my actions. Now, I'm thankful you bailed me out, but those are my men back there, so excuse me while I go return the favor."

Elaine grabbed him and kissed him passionately. Marcus was stunned by the action. He pulled her in closer before she pulled away.

"I… I'm sorry, you just… when you talk to me like that, it makes me so… well, let me show you."

Elaine grabbed his hand and slid it underneath her skirt. Her panties were moist to the touch. Surprised, he looked into her eyes.

"I want to feel you, Marcus."

"What, here? Now?"

"Right now."

Elaine opened her silver sedan and climbed into the back seat. Marcus scanned the area. Before he was finished, he felt the lace of her baby blue thong hitting his chest.

"Are you gonna stand there or are you gonna come and fuck me?"

She didn't have to ask twice. He'd been wanting her since she promised to give him breakfast, a back rub and a blowjob. He climbed inside of the car, closed the door and unfastened his pants. As soon as he could get them down, his hard dick was ready to enter her soft moist walls.

"Damn, that's wet," he moaned. He took several slow strokes, each one pushing deeper inside of her to feel the depth of her pussy.

She kissed him and looked him in the eyes. "Don't be nice, soldier, not tonight."

Marcus began drilling her with his emboldened dick.

In the heat of their passion was an unspoken agreement. She wouldn't give him the falsity of an insincere moan. He would have to earn them. In no uncertain terms, she would only be satisfied by his best efforts.

The harder he fucked her, the louder she moaned. Each time she said *fuck me harder*, he would meet the challenge. Until she said *that's it* and then stopped speaking as her moans turned into high-pitched squeals. He knew someone had to hear them by now. He didn't care. Why would he?

I want them to hear.

He held nothing back with each thrust, and she salivated. His condition was irrelevant. He was alive, and he was going to fuck her better than anyone has ever fucked her and she was going to tell the world with each moan.

"Oh, my god y— " Her screams hit a falsetto pitch he'd never heard before.

He was sweating profusely as his black T-shirt clung to him the more he sweat. He punished her pussy as best as he'd ever done. All of his frustration, strength, endurance, and compassion were being called upon in this moment as the force of the car rocking set off the car alarm, blaring in concert with her screams, and his hips making a thunderous clap each time he entered her moist pussy.

"I'm coming!" she howled at the top of her lungs as her eyes rolled to the back of her head. She was in orgasmic bliss. It turned him on as she bit his pectoral muscle.

The pain, combined with her pleasure, forced him close to his own climax as she gripped his back, tearing his shirt and clawing away at his shoulders. The lustful nature of their encounter brought him to a climax as his seed began to fill her pussy, warming her insides. Their lust for each other was quenched.

"I've... never....ever... been fucked like this... ever. You're a god," she panted.

The words made him proud. Not because of the sex itself, but because he'd done what he'd set out to do. He gave it his all and willed it to reality.

In this moment of his fleeting life, he felt immortal, and an immortal could do anything. Including saving his men, and just maybe even cheating death itself. He caught his breath and looked at Elaine. She was still panting.

"I'm not done fighting, Elaine."

"I never... doubted it... Bravo Fights," she said, still catching her breath.

"Bravo Fights," he nodded.

She kissed him gently and looked into his eyes and smiled seductively. "Welcome back, Sergeant Winters."

The more he examined her eyes, the more he found echoes of himself. His pride had kicked in and he had her to thank for it. He realized in this moment he'd never felt more connected to her. Good or bad, she was always there when he needed her.

"Elaine, I don't know if I've done a good job of telling you how much you mean to me. To my overall wellbeing. Thank you for—"

Tap, tap, tap.

There was a knock on the door. Marcus scrambled to gather himself, peering out the window.

"Shit, it's General Reese."

8

THE GENERAL

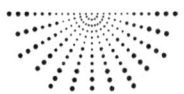

*T*ap, tap, tap.

"One second, General." Marcus quickly fastened his clothing while Elaine found the remote to the car alarm. Marcus got out of the car and stood at attention to buy Elaine some time to get dressed.

"General Reese, sir!" he said. His previous bravado was now gone. A few moments earlier, he didn't care who'd heard them. Now, he was embarrassed that one of those people was his former commander.

Reese lit a cigar and puffed on it, and after a spell, responded, "At ease, soldier, though I should keep you standing at attention since you seem to enjoy it so much, you decided to let everyone in the parking lot know it."

Marcus nervously chuckled at the reference. "Well, I'm a civilian now, sir. Just showing some due respect."

The general took another puff of his cigar and raised his voice to make sure anyone within earshot heard him. "Whether enlisted or civilian, I still expect people who have, or currently serve, under my command to know how to act on a military base."

"Understood, sir. It won't happen again, sir."

Marcus was certain the comment was as much for Elaine as it was for him.

He glanced towards the car as she was buttoning her blouse while trying to remain in the shadows. The general realized the same, and motioned Marcus away from the car.

"Walk with me, Winters. Let's talk."

The two strolled towards the military police station, the general deep in thought. Marcus was impressed that the general kept himself in good physical shape despite being in his late 60s; his hair was salt-and-pepper, and he wore glasses now but he was the consummate professional, a prototype for all Army officers: fit and focused at all times.

Marcus concentrated on the latter. He knew the man well enough to know that, when he puffed on a cigar, he was deep in thought.

After a spell, Marcus asked. "Something on your mind, sir?"

"I was processing Jackson's preliminary paperwork when Staff Sergeant Revis burst in my door saying he'd been assaulted by a Sergeant Marcus Winters. I thought to myself *that's a name I haven't heard in a long time*. I told Revis there had to be some mistake, because the Sergeant Winters I know is the textbook soldier.

"But as I'm defending this slanderous account of the soldier I know, I get the MP daily intake manifest email and on the list it says that Sergeant Gibson, Sergeant Hayes, and – you guessed it – Sergeant Marcus Winters, were being detained for a violent altercation. So, I said there's no way it's the Marcus Winters I know. Someone is slandering the man's good name. Let me take a drive down here and catch him in the act.

"So, I get here. There's Gibson and Hayes, but no Winters. I said *ah ha*! Now I have my first clue, because the real Sergeant Winters wouldn't have left his men behind in a cell.

"I spring Hayes and Gibson and ask where this impostor could be, and they didn't know, but when we got outside, all I could hear was a car alarm about thirty paces away and what sounded like screams for God. Hayes tells me you're probably in the car's backseat... how did he put it? Ah yes, folding Corporal Holt like fresh laundry. And when

I get to the car, sure enough, it's you, smelling like tequila and unwashed ass," the general said dryly.

"Sir, I—"

"Relax, Winters. I'm just busting your chops. Not about the unwashed ass comment. You need to go home and take a shower."

"Yes, sir, will do. But I doubt you came all the way down here to talk about my hygiene."

"No, son, I didn't." The admiral said as he puffed his cigar. "I heard how you handled the Jackson incident. Sounds like if Revis hadn't interfered, we'd still have a soldier with us."

"Sir, Revis was only doing what he felt was right. He had a base to protect, I can't—"

"Revis is a nincompoop," General Reese said.

Marcus chuckled at the word he hadn't heard since he was active military. He nodded at General Reese's assessment as he continued.

"I also heard some deeply troubling news about you, personally. I'm sorry, son."

Marcus knew he was referring to his illness. He'd tried to keep it under wraps, but nothing is private on a military base.

"It is troubling, sir, but a Bravo man fights until his dying breath."

"That they do, son. I have to admit, Bravo company doesn't have the same pride it did when you were here. You were – excuse me, *are* – a hell of a soldier."

"Thank you, sir."

"That's why I want to talk to you and Hayes about your initiative."

"Initiative, sir?"

"Well, while you were testing the suspension of that Nissan Maxima over there, Hayes, Gibson, and I were talking about your concept, Brothers in Arms."

Marcus looked up and saw Ryan and Shanice both mimicking sexual acts to tease him.

He gave them the middle finger as the general continued.

"So you want to help soldiers deal with the trauma war brings and help them transition back to their lives stateside?"

"Yes, sir. I think Jackson's death today was a wake-up call for me, and I hope for a few like-minded individuals. When we go to war, we're with our brothers and sisters in arms, which is why I wanted to call the organization Brothers in Arms. It's all still in the brainstorming phase, and nothing's set in concrete yet."

The general took another toke of his cigar, exhaled, and replied, "Well, I gotta admit I like the sound of it. Other than today's shenanigans, you are without question the finest soldier I know, and I couldn't think of a better candidate to spearhead a project like this. If you like, I'll authorize a trial run of your initiative on base."

Marcus was stunned by the words as he paused momentarily, processing the events of the day. "Sir, with all due respect, the Army almost never moves this quickly unless we're at war."

The general dropped his cigar on the ground and ashed it with his boot.

"Winters, I've served my country for over fifty years and, from what I can tell, I don't think it's getting better. It used to be that a man served his country and came home and picked up a normal life, but after Vietnam everything changed. Drug use, spousal abuse and, yes, suicide, all skyrocketed. As far as I'm concerned, we are at war, Winters. The battlefield is the mind.

"Hayes pointed out an interesting fact to me earlier. You're the only leader that's ever been under my command that hasn't lost a soldier, which makes you the perfect candidate to help these soldiers transition back to civilian lives. The thing I need to know is, if you're interested in serving your country one last time."

Marcus turned to face the general, encouraged by his words, and asked, "When do we start?"

9

THE CORPORAL

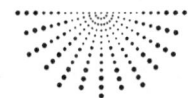

"Seventy-five, seventy-six, seventy-seven."

Marcus huffed. Today was a big day and, for the first time in a while, being sick wasn't on his mind. He had somewhere to be, and it was where he wanted to be.

He missed the Army. He loved seeing the new recruits getting ready to be transformed; some for the better, some for the worse. But he was excited to have a reason to be on base. He'd been feeling aimless even before the diagnosis, but afterwards he was all but reckless.

He had to meet Ryan to go over what they'd talk about, and how to break the ice with the guys. It was important for him to set the right tone, and he wanted to be sure he was up to the task.

Although he had no discernable proof, he'd convinced himself that being physically fit gave him the best fighting chance to stave off the worst of his condition. "Ninety-nine, one hundred," he said as he finished the push-ups and hopped in the shower.

Today was the day. Brothers in Arms was officially in business, and their first contract was at his old military base. His mind was racing.

When he got out of the shower, he stared at his closet. He settled on the shirt he wore every time he came back from deployment, the shirt he would greet Kendra in. Marcus lifted the shirt up, realizing he'd lost some weight since the diagnosis, so the shirt was baggy. It didn't matter. He wanted to wear it.

This shirt was meaningful, but his favorite item was a black metallic bracelet Kendra had given him as a Valentine's gift when they'd first started dating. It had been months since they'd broken up, but he still wore the bracelet because it calmed him.

"Babe, what are you doing?" Elaine asked as he was holding the shirt in the air.

"Trying to decide what to wear. I want to strike the right tone. I don't want to overdress, but I don't want to underdress."

Elaine laid on the bed, her satin blue robe slipping to reveal her right nipple.

"So, you wanna be one of the guys, but also want the guys to know you're in charge, am I right?"

"Exactly! What do you think about this shirt?"

He put the shirt on. It was a little big, but it still looked good. Elaine hopped up and walked over to the full-sized mirror he was standing in front of. She wrapped her arms around his shoulders.

"You know, I've always liked this shirt on you. You look sexy in it. But I figured you'd need help for your big day, so I took the liberty of doing this." She kissed him and walked over to the closet, pulling out a box. Marcus watched her as she grinned ear to ear. "Well, open it!"

She clasped her hands and smiled as he opened the box. Inside was a forest-green T-shirt accompanied by black stonewashed jeans.

He replaced his shirt with her gift. It felt good and fit perfectly.

He glanced at Elaine, who was bubbling in delight, and then back at the shirt. It wasn't his usual style. He didn't care for v-neck shirts, but this one looked nice. Still, a part of him wanted to wear the other shirt because Kendra had given it to him.

His hesitation caught Elaine's attention. "You don't like it."

Marcus examined the shirt. It looked good, felt good. Much better than the shirt he'd originally chosen. In a way it reflected his life as of late. This was a new chapter in his fleeting life, one that didn't include Kendra. Elaine had been good to him. It was time to let Kendra go.

He turned to her and, with a grand smile, replied, "I love it."

Elaine squealed and clapped gleefully. She wrapped her arms around him. Even if he didn't like the shirt, he knew there was no way he could say so now. She'd thought of him, and that meant a lot.

"Check out the right shoulder sleeve," she said.

He glanced down and noticed on the edge of the sleeve a fabric similar to the color of the jeans, with the words 'Bravo Fights' written in the same green color of the shirt.

Damn, she really pays attention to me.

The outfit was exactly the look he was going for, and he wasn't sure how she knew what he needed at this moment, but she did.

He took her hands and looked into her eyes. "Thank you, Elaine. Seriously, thank you for everything."

She kissed him and slapped him on his bare ass cheek. "Get dressed, soldier. Chow is cooking. Being on time is being fifteen minutes late, so you have to get out the door, pronto." Marcus nodded, and Elaine went back to the kitchen.

As he finished getting dressed, the outfit grew on him. He looked good and felt confident, and although he wasn't taking a piece of Kendra with him, he was taking Bravo company, and Elaine.

After getting dressed, he went into the kitchen. Elaine, still in her robe, had made his favorite meal: an egg-white turkey bacon omelet with a side of waffles. "This looks good, babe," he said as he sat down to eat the food.

It all tasted amazing. Since they'd been practically living together, Elaine had really improved her already-impressive cooking skills. Marcus would joke with her from time to time and say, 'You finally figured out how seasoning works,' each time she would make a meal he loved. It was their banter. This meal was one of her best. He appreciated her effort. She was good to him.

"Babe, this hit the spot," he clamored, feasting on what felt like a king's breakfast.

Marcus was about to leave when Elaine stopped him. "Before you go, can I say goodbye to my—"

"Oh no, we're not starting that up. Being on time is being late, remember?"

"Let me just look at it," she pleaded.

Marcus put up what little resistance he could in a halfhearted response. "Elaine, I gotta go. I can't be late on the first day."

"Just pull it out so I can see it. I just want to see it, that's all."

He knew better, but looking into her ocean-blue eyes, he couldn't resist.

As he unbuttoned and unzipped his pants, he watched as Elaine's pout turn into a seductive grin.

"There he is. Hi, Mr. Lumberjack."

"You're still going with that name?"

"I'm working on a few," she said as she walked over and touched his firming dick.

He smiled and asked, "Such as?"

"Well, there's Mr. Lumberjack."

"Okay."

"There's my little battle buddy."

"Definitely not that one."

"And there's my straw."

"Straw? Why that one?" Marcus said.

Elaine smiled, going to her knees. She looked up innocently as his dick stood at full attention. "Let me show you."

She licked the tip of his dick. It bounced at the sensation of her tongue. She then slowly licked the palm of her right hand and wrapped it around his vessel, stroking it slowly.

"Damn," he moaned as his knees weakened. The pleasure of her moist hand rubbing his dick made his knees weaken.

She licked her left palm and wrapped it around his dick and in one motion, began slowly sucking his dick, twisting her hands as she further pushed his rock-hard dick into her mouth.

He looked at the clock. He was going to be late, but he couldn't resist her.

She went deeper, picking up the pace of her suction as the warmth of her tongue further hardened his dick. She went deeper and deeper each time as he rolled his eyes to the back of his head.

"Damn, that's good," he moaned.

She stopped suddenly, startling him. "Wha... what? Why did you stop?"

"Because, like you said, you gotta go. I don't want you to be late. Do you like the nickname?"

Marcus turned her around and lifted her robe, sliding his already erect manhood inside of her.

Elaine gasped. "What are you—"

"I just need a few strokes."

His impulses took over. He rapidly started to drill into her pussy as it pulsated around his dick. He didn't want to be late, but her oral skills had worked him up, and if he didn't release his urges, there was no way he'd be able to concentrate.

Elaine leaned over the counter to receive him fully as he pushed his dick deep into her. Their combined fluids dripped onto the floor. She was so wet that it didn't take long for him to cum.

"Oh god," he moaned as he released his hot load into her.

He pulled out of her and took a moment to catch his breath.

Elaine turned around and got on her knees, licking his now-limp tool. He was exhausted, but her tongue felt wonderful.

"There, good as new," she said with a smirk.

He shook his head at her freak nature.

She stood up as he zipped his pants. And slapped him on his ass cheek again. "Now get out of here soldier, you're gonna be late."

Marcus sighed as he walked out the door. Before he left, he turned. "Elaine?

"Yeah, babe?"

"If I have a vote, I definitely like the straw."

10

THE SERGEANT (FIRST CLASS)

"Winters, you're late," Hayes said as Marcus walked into the conference room three minutes before eight. Although the event started at eight, his unspoken rule of being fifteen to thirty minutes early was already broken. Everything in the Army started right on time.

"Traffic was bad. Won't happen again," he responded.

Hayes persisted and walked toward him. "Listen, if you're not up to this, say so now. No shame in being sick."

"Like I said, Hayes, it won't happen again."

Ryan nodded as the last soldiers walked into the building. He examined the group, over thirty men and a handful of women, most of them he'd never met before. He'd gotten off to a shaky start, but now it was time to deliver.

"Bravo doesn't fail, Bravo doesn't quit, Bravo fights," he muttered to himself. His battle cry before taking on any large task. His nerves were steady. He was ready.

"My name is Sergeant Marcus Winters. I served two tours in Afghanistan. They decorated me with several medals, including the purple heart, and I'd never lost a soldier until two weeks ago, when Darrell Jackson committed suicide on this base. Also, I'm dying and it's with my final breaths that I want to do everything in my power to help all of you make better lives for yourself after the military. Because I know how hard it is to transition."

As Marcus continued, he realized the soldiers were attentive and engaged, which only made him more comfortable and confident. He talked on a variety of topics: his life after the military, his affair, and how to turn off the rage he felt for being wired to kill at a moment's notice.

There were several soldiers who eventually broke into tears with their own stories about the difficulty of transitioning back home. Ryan shared details on his suicide attempt. What was supposed to be one hour lasted nearly two, and as the event came to a head for the week, Marcus realized that helping others had always been his purpose.

As the event ended, he shook each soldier's hand, all of whom thanked him and signed up for next week's session.

It was the best thing he'd done since leaving the military. For the first time in years, he felt he had purpose.

As he and Hayes finished cleaning up, he heard a knock on the door.

"Hey, babe! How did it go?"

"Uh, hey, Elaine. What are you doing here?"

"Just checking on you, seeing how the session went before I start work myself," she said as she wrapped her arms around his shoulders.

Embarrassed by the affection, Marcus quickly removed them. "Babe, look, I appreciate you coming, but let's try to limit the PDA while we're on base."

"You gotta be kidding me," she responded.

Ryan interjected, "I'm with Elaine on this one. Now you're worried about PDA? 'Cause a military parking lot is pretty freaking public."

Marcus cut his gaze to his friend, who raised his hands in concession. "I want to keep it professional. Is that okay with you?"

"Marcus, just a few weeks ago you were in the backseat of my car letting the entire state of Virginia know what we have is not professional, so why the sudden urge to act like we're not together?"

Marcus pulled her into a corner, away from Hayes' active listening ears and continued, "Some of these men come to you for therapy, outside of what I'm trying to build. I need them to know we're not pillow-talking about their issues. I just really want this to go well."

"Are you sure that's all?"

"Yeah, why do you ask that?"

"Because, you and Gibson—"

"Oh, here we go again. This has nothing to do with Shanice. Like I've said before, we are just friends, and quite frankly, I wouldn't have this opportunity if it wasn't for Gibson."

"What opportunity?" Gibson asked as she entered the conference room.

Marcus turned to greet his friend as Elaine rolled her eyes. "Gib! I was just—"

"I'll catch her up to speed," Ryan interrupted. "Winters doesn't want anyone to know they're clapping ass-cheeks, and he was trying to tell Holt that when she got jealous because she thinks you're trying to steal her boyfriend, and that's when you walked in."

Marcus glanced at Elaine, who was stone-faced as Gibson responded.

"Well, first of all, that's a dick move, Marcus. Half the base already heard you guys the other day, so your secret's out. And secondly, Elaine, being threatened by my presence? Well, that's understandable. I mean, if I were someone else and felt I had to compete with me, I'd be insecure too," Gibson joked, adding to the building tension.

Marcus shook his head, unsure of what to say or do next as Elaine responded, "I don't think I'm competing with anybody."

"That's good. I'm glad you tell yourself that. Makes it sound more convincing when you say it out loud."

"You know what? Fu—"

"Ladies! That's enough. Go back to your corners. Sheesh," Marcus called out.

"You see? What'd I tell ya? I'm so fine, even women want me. Sorry, Elaine, I'm strictly dickly, but for you I could make an exception. Maybe you can join us?"

"Gib!" Marcus exclaimed, cutting off the banter as Ryan doubled over in laughter.

Shanice looked at Elaine, who was turning red with anger. "Relax, Elaine, no one wants your man. But I do need him, desperately. Right now, in fact."

"Gib!" Marcus yelled, cutting her off again while she and Ryan continued to laugh at Elaine's expense.

"No, seriously, General Reese wants a report on how things went today, and since I'm the commanding officer in charge, that would make me your boss, and I take my job very seriously."

She winked in his direction, still getting a rile out of Elaine, who was beet-red.

Marcus, hoping to defuse the situation, responded, "Not helping at all, Gib."

He then turned to Elaine, who was visibly upset, and put his arm on her shoulder. "Babe, it's part of the job. I won't be long, I promise."

"No, it's fine. I'm an adult, and I get that you have stuff to do. I just wanted to drop your meds off since you forgot them this morning. You have a good time with whatever you're doing."

"Elaine!" Marcus called for her, but it was too late. She had already walked away.

11

BUFFALO SOLIDER

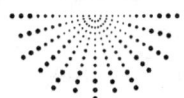

"*T*he Brothers in Arms liaison briefing between Staff Sergeant Shanice Gibson and Sergeant Marcus Winters will hereby commence!" Gibson shouted as she took her second shot of Uncle Nearest whiskey.

Marcus smiled at his childhood friend. He had known Shanice since the ninth grade. They'd even joined the military together. She was his original ride or die. No one knew Marcus better.

"That one stings," Marcus winced, holding his neck to help the pain subside.

"Don't be a pussy, Winters."

"You do know I'm dying?"

"No excuses, finish strong," she replied.

She lifted the third shot in the air before continuing. "So we took one shot for Jackson, one shot for Brothers in Arms. What's the third one for?"

Marcus took a sip of his beer as he thought about her question and then, without hesitating, picked up his glass and joined her in the toast.

"To the two baddest motherfuckers to ever join Bravo Company!"

Marcus shouted as they took the final shot. The pair banged the table as Tennessee Whiskey played on the jukebox.

He glanced at Shanice, who clearly had something on her mind.

She finally made eye contact with him and, without changing her expression, asked, "So, is dating a crazy white girl some kind of bucket list thing?"

"Elaine is not crazy."

"If you think she's not crazy, then you're crazy."

"Gib..."

"If that's the case, why didn't you just tell her we were hanging out today?"

Marcus took a sip of his beer before responding, "She can be a little much. I just wanted to kick it with you, no distractions."

"Well, as long as you're happy, I guess that works for me," she laughed.

It was good to be around her again. He knew her well enough to know she wanted to know more about his diagnosis, but she wouldn't ask. She knew him well enough to know he didn't want to talk about it. He appreciated the unspoken understanding.

When he'd been dating Kendra, and Shanice was engaged, their friendship had been hard to maintain. Now it was as if they were picking up right where they left off. It felt good to do that without Elaine hovering around, or Hayes' off-color jokes.

"I missed you, Gib," Marcus said as he punched her in the arm.

She slapped him upside the head playfully in return. "It's been a long time. But I would've thought I'd made the shortlist about you and Kendra breaking up. I know that had to be hard on you."

"It's brutal, to be honest. There are days I wake up and, if I'm being real, I tear up thinking about her."

"Why didn't you contact me?"

"And say what? The last time I saw you, you told me that Rodney didn't like our friendship because he thought we were too close."

"Rodney was insecure, and I was wrong. Seeing you and Elaine is eerily similar to that."

Marcus finished his beer before waving the bartender over for another round. He let out a quiet belch and replied, "Look, Gib, when you and Rodney decided that our friendship was interfering with your relationship, I respected it and pulled back. Once I started dating Kendra, I even understood it. Right now, I'm gonna ask you to do the same. Elaine is, if nothing else, reliable. I could think of worse ways to spend my last days. I'm happy."

The two were quiet before a spell, allowing his words to sink in.

Finally, Gibson asked, "So, what happened with you and Kendra?"

"Did I not just say I'm not talking about my relationship?"

"Your current relationship. Not your ex relationship, unless there's unresolved—"

"I've got a better idea. Tell me why you're back without Rodney."

Gibson flipped him off playfully and, as the drinks arrived, took her vodka-and-Red Bull and downed it before asking for another. After a long pause, she said, "You know, they say people grow apart. It's probably the textbook definition of what happened with us."

Shanice took a long sip of her drink and continued. "I've been to Istanbul, Spain, Russia, Morocco. He's just trying to get to the state capital. I speak eight different languages, and he just wants to buy a set of thirty-inch rims and listen to J Cole. He's settled, and I want more for myself. I need adventure. I need the outdoors."

"So, are you coming back to run the base? Because that's a step in the wrong direction if you're talking about action."

"Not exactly. Remember when we were overseas, and we did that joint op with the CIA?"

"Yeah, you went undercover like some female James Bond. To this day, I still have no idea what happened."

"Well, let's just say I impressed a few people along the way. I'm doing this job right now, but I've interviewed for another." Shanice took another sip and smiled.

Marcus' eyes widened. He knew that look all too well. She could never keep a secret from him. "No fucking way. Langley?"

"Keep your goddamn voice down, Marcus."

"I'm sorry, it's not every day you meet someone who's gonna work for the CI—"

"Marcus!"

"I'm sorry, it's just... Wow, I'm happy for you, congratulations."

"I haven't gotten the job yet, but we'll see if it happens."

"Gib, when have you failed at anything? And you've wanted this since we were kids. It's in the bag. Congratulations,"

Her smile stretched wide across her face, exposing her pearly-white teeth. She was genuinely happy, and he was genuinely happy for her. She was never one to settle. Since they were kids, she'd built her life her way.

That was Shanice Gibson, in a nutshell.

"So when do you find out?" he asked, still excited about the news.

"I don't know all the specifics, but I know it's gonna be a field assignment. If I get in, I basically become a ghost here. All of my records will be erased from public record. I effectively won't exist."

Marcus nodded in understanding. The liquor was taking effect, but he had a somber moment. He realized that, whenever she left, it would be the last time he saw her.

He took a sip of the beer and then looked her in the eyes. "Gib, you've been the best friend a man could have in this life. I'm always gonna—"

"None of that sentimental shit, Winters. I know where you stand, and you know where I stand," she said, cutting him off.

As the waitress returned with their fourth shot, he handed her one and lifted the other in the air. "To family."

The pair smiled and finished their liquor.

"Alright, so what happened with you and Kendra?"

Marcus rolled his eyes. He didn't want to talk about it, but he knew their earlier unspoken agreement did not protect this area of his life. He finally relented and replied, "I don't know, Gib. Leaving the military was a mistake for me. I truly loved Kendra, and I wanted to support her in her career."

"I know how much you did for her. That's why I was shocked."

"Well, once we got down to Houston, I felt lost. I didn't have the military. I didn't have any real purpose. I was invisible. When we first got there, she had all these corporate events we had to attend. I didn't know much about suits, or the stock market, or whatever it was they did up there, but I tried to fit in. One day, she told me she was going by herself. That shouldn't have been a big deal, but it bothered me. Made me feel like I disappointed her."

"So, you stepped out on her?"

"I did," he admitted reluctantly.

Shanice took a sip of her drink and examined his face. He could feel her assessing him. He never could hide the truth from her. After a moment, she guessed, "With someone she knew?"

Marcus took a sip of his beer, his silence confirming her suspicions.

"You fucked a neighbor?"

"A coworker."

"Unbelievable! You men are such fuckin' assholes." she exclaimed as she shook her head in disapproval. Marcus could tell the liquor was affecting her.

"Gib, let me expl— "

"I don't want to hear it. This woman had to fight to have a seat in the world that you all built, and the moment she didn't have time to tend to your bruised ego, you go fuck her coworker."

Her words stung. But that was Gibson. She spoke her mind, and he respected her for it.

He heaved a sigh and replied, "Look, I wasn't trying to fuck her. It just kinda happened."

"What, did she just come to your house, knock on the door and say 'let me fuck you'?"

"Well, yeah, actually, that's exactly how it happened. I was at home, just mindin' my own business. One day, she knocks on the door—"

"It doesn't matter, Marcus! Look, I know you were going through a transition, but did you ever stop to think about how much pressure Kendra was under? New city, new job, people thinking she's some kind of diversity hire, or somehow her brain doesn't function as well because she has tits, having to constantly prove herself. All of that while dealing with your cheating ass. Do you know what that had to do to her self-esteem?"

"Gib, are you talking about Kendra or yourself right now?"

"Does it matter? I swear, men have to be the stupidest of all of God's creatures. Do you have any idea how hard it is for a woman to open up and trust a man? She's letting him into her body, her heart, her spirit, and I don't care what you think happened. A woman erases you from her heart only when you've left her no choice. Now, maybe she could've handled things a little better, but if you ask me, you got off easy. I swear, you men ain't shit. You're always looking for pussy, but don't know what to do with it once you have it. The truth of the matter is, if you actually had a pussy, you'd fold under the pressure of carrying it around every day."

Marcus scoffed at his friend's menacing words and then replied, "So, I'm gonna ignore the fact that some of that had to be about Rodney, and you clearly needed to get it off your chest."

"What? No, I—"

"Let me stop you right there, because I know you just as well as you know me, and I know when you're deflecting. But you're right, I should've handled it better. You know me, I'm not the cheating type. I don't know why I did it. I just wanted to feel something, you know? Hell, she was too busy to realize it was even happening. I don't think she knows to this day. I mean, even when we got back here, all she wanted to do was go back to Houston. So, me and Elaine started up. But she only found out about that after she'd been overseas getting her knees pushed back by some dark-skinned, bald-headed motherfucker she met on vacation and decided she wanted to be with him."

"So, wait, she doesn't know you slept with her coworker?"

"After everything I just said, that's what you're stuck on?"

"Answer me, Marcus. Does she know or not?"

"I don't know. I mean, I haven't spoken to her since she left."

"Call her."

"What?"

"Call her. Right now," she repeated enthusiastically.

Marcus reached for his phone, quickly grabbing it off the counter before Shanice could grab it. "I'm not calling Kendra."

"Marcus, if you don't give me your phone, I'm gonna break your collarbone in three different places."

"I'm not calling her, Shanice."

Gibson scrubbed her hands across her face, clearly frustrated with him. She took a deep breath. "You cannot let the woman you say you love walk around completely clueless. You owe her this. Call her and tell her."

Marcus put the phone in his back pocket. "I'm not calling her or telling her anything."

Shanice leaned back and smiled. "Fine, you don't want to call her? That's cool. I'm gonna tell your momma."

Marcus' eyes widened at her threat, causing him to knock over his beer.

As Shanice scrolled through her contacts, Marcus grabbed her hand and looked her squarely in her eyes, exposing the depths of his soul. "Shanice, I'm begging you, please do not call my mom. As far as she knows, everything is just fine. I don't want her to deal with any more stress, especially not this crap."

Shanice held the phone in her other hand and weighed his words as she looked into his eyes. "You haven't told her about your diagnosis, have you?"

He pulled his hand away as his eyes shifted downward, confirming her suspicions.

"Marcus Bernard Winters the Second, please tell me you told your mother that her oldest son has six months to live."

"Like I said, I didn't want to stress her."

"You have to be the most ignorant son of a... Have you told anyone? Paul? The colonel?"

"No, I have not told my brother, Paul, and as far as my pops goes, I think you know the answer to that."

"That's bullshit, Marcus! Why wouldn't you tell your family what's going on with you? I don't even recognize you right now."

Marcus slammed his hand on the table and pointed at Shanice in frustration. "That right there is what's wrong with me! I am so fucking sick and tired of living up to the world's expectations. Do you know I didn't even want to go into the military? I did it because the great Colonel Marcus Bernard Winters Senior decreed it. I've made every decision in my life for everyone else but me. So, yeah, I'm not worried about what you or anyone else thinks about my final days, because they are *my* final days and I want to spend them in peace, not feeling like I didn't live up to yours or anyone's expectations. This is who I am, and I don't care if it's a better version or worse version than the man you knew. I just want to be happy, Shanice."

Marcus picked up a glass of water and took a sip while he tried to calm himself.

Shanice nodded and, after a while, responded. "I'm gonna ignore the fact you just sat here and asked me if I knew you didn't want to go to the military, because clearly you must be sick. And I get that you've made a life of living up to people's expectations. But I know you, Marcus, and not telling your family, me, or Kendra? Confiding in Holt? I'm supposed to think you're just fine? 'Cause I don't."

"Well, I am."

"Cut the shit, Marcus, this is me you're talking to. You're scared."

"What? I've served two tours in Afghanistan in heavy combat. I'm not afraid of dying."

"I don't think you're afraid of dying, Marcus. You're afraid that when you die, you'll be a disappointment in the eyes of the colonel."

The words stunned Marcus, his nostril flaring. She'd hit the nerve with a sniper's accuracy, and his face all but confirmed she was right.

He'd had enough quality time with his old friend for one day. He chugged the remaining water. "First of all, you don't know a goddamn thing about me anymore. I may have looked up to my father as a boy, but that was before I realized we were all just pawns in his quest for political domination. He wanted a soldier, not a son, so like any soldier, he'll find out about my death when the clergy arrives at their home. Now, if you'll excuse me, I'm gonna go home to my crazy, white girlfriend. Now, have a good day."

HE WALKED out of the door without looking back. He got in his car and blared No Role Models by J Cole.

"Gibson's an asshole," he muttered to himself.

Distracted by her truths, he sped down the highway. As he was driving, his hand started shaking. "Come on, Winters, hold it together."

Suddenly his arm went limp.

"Oh, not now!" he yelled.

He was having a spasm, driving fifty miles an hour with no way to control his truck.

He glanced ahead as his truck veered into the opposite lane. A large truck was oncoming. His leg was shaking as he heard the horn in front of him. His pulse was racing, the car was drifting; there was nothing he could do.

He draped his body on the wheel of the car, hoping to move it. The car swerved hard into the ditch.

12
NAME, RANK & SERIAL NUMBER

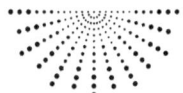

"*Y*ou okay, buddy?"

Marcus tried to get his bearings, the blow from the airbag distorting him. The truck driver was peering into his window.

Marcus scanned the area. To his surprise, he was not only alive, but had avoided a major accident. It seemed the truck driver had stopped in time, and had positioned his vehicle to stop any traffic from getting into what would have been a head-on collision.

His senses were returning to him.

His car had ended up in a shallow ditch. His off-road tires would be good enough to get the car out. He wanted to get out to inspect the damage.

"Don't move, you might be hurt."

"Is everyone all right?"

"Yeah, I stopped once I saw you swerving into my lane and turned. You just crashed into this ditch. Did you lose power?"

"Think so. I couldn't control it," Marcus said, getting out of the car despite the trucker's warning.

He looked at the damage. There was a slight scratch on the front fender, but other than that, it was fine. He knew death was coming for him, but he was relieved that today wasn't the day.

"Man, you're lucky to be alive."

"I was just thinking that. Thank you for your quick actions. You probably saved my life."

Marcus shook the man's hand and then realized the man was inspecting him.

"Hey buddy, are you okay? Your eyes are red."

He saw through the subtle nature of the question. *Have you been drinking?*

He wasn't sure if the trucker had smelled alcohol on his breath, but he kept his distance. "The airbag did a number on me, I'm a little disoriented. Hit me square in the face."

"Yeah? Looked like you were having a seizu—"

"Like I said, I'm fine. Just thankful no one got hurt."

"Marcus!"

He turned around and spotted Elaine getting out of her car, rushing towards him.

He glanced behind her and saw a military police patrol vehicle stopping and two officers got out of the truck. Marcus met Elaine halfway and hugged her.

"Marcus are you alright?" she asked.

He pulled her in close and whispered, "I'm fine. I had an episode in the car and lost control, but I've been drinking, and I think this guy is starting to question if that was the cause, and now the MPs are coming."

Elaine hugged him tighter. "Okay, first I'm going to get you out of here, and then we're going straight to medical." Elaine released him and headed back up to the military police officers and began explaining.

After a minute, he could see Elaine laughing and handing something to one of the officers. She walked back to Marcus, who had put more distance between him and the truck driver.

"The MPs are from Bravo company. They said as long as everyone else is okay, you have nothing to worry about. I'll get them to write up a report later, but we need to get you to Dr. Packard. I'm driving your truck there, and one officer is going to drive mine, breaking at least four state and federal laws by my count, but we should be good."

Marcus smiled as the truck driver started to walk towards him.

He handed Elaine the keys. "Let's get out of here."

13

ON THE DOUBLE

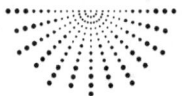

"How much longer?" he asked as they waited on the results of the latest test.

"As long as it takes," Elaine said coldly.

He knew she was upset, but whether it was his accident, the drinking, or breaking several laws to help him, he wasn't entirely sure.

Marcus watched as she paced back and forth, scowling at him, then looking away. He decided he wouldn't say anything unless she did. After a few minutes, she finally caved.

"I hate this, Marcus."

"What is it exactly that you hate?" he asked.

"You know what I mean. Her."

"The singer?"

"No, smart ass. Gibson. I hate that she's here."

Marcus rolled his eyes. "I almost died, and this is what's troubling you?"

"It's her fault you almost died. She's a bad influence on you, Marcus."

"Elaine, I've known Gibson since I was fourteen."

"And that's the problem, isn't it? Because every time she's around, you turn into a high schooler."

Her words fed the already-growing anger he'd been suppressing as he sat up and looked at her sternly. "What did you say to me?"

Elaine quickly picked up on his tone and softened her own while holding her ground.

"I didn't mean it like that. I meant— You know what I mean, babe. She's trouble. Hayes is bad enough, but every time Gibson is around, nothing good happens to you. I don't know why you can't see that."

Marcus looked at her blankly. He shook his head in disbelief. "Elaine, let's be clear about something. Gibson is like a sister to me, on and off the battlefield. Remember that mission where I saved your life? Well, Gibson saved mine at least twice that same day. How you feel, or don't feel, about her is out of my control. I expect you to respect my friendship with Gib."

Elaine was about to respond when there was a tap at the door.

"Come in," Marcus bellowed.

Dr. Packard walked in, his eyes on his clipboard.

Marcus was relieved to see him. There were worse fates than being at the doctor's office, and right now arguing with Elaine about Gibson was at the top of the list.

He watched the doctor, who never made eye contact with either of them, fix his glasses. After a thorough examination of the clipboard, he enquired, "How are you feeling, Mr. Winters?"

"Feel fine, doc. Tell me, what's the damage?"

The doctor shuffled through his notes and said, "Well, the good news is your overall numbers are much better than expected, but there is a significant increase in your cortisone levels."

"Is that why I had an episode?"

"Of course it is," Elaine chimed in. "Tell him, Dr. Packard, he needs rest and—"

"Elaine, I'm talking to Dr. Packard. Let him do his job, please," Marcus implored, cutting her off.

The doctor glanced at Elaine, then back at Marcus. Then down to his keyboard. He repositioned his glasses, cleared his throat, and continued. "Well, you should avoid stressful situations. I'm going to keep your dosage where it is for the time being becau—"

"Doctor, don't you think you should increase his dosage? So we can be sure he doesn't have any more issues?" Elaine interjected.

Marcus had had enough. "Damn it, Elaine, let the man do his job," he barked.

The doctor raised his hand to calm the growing tension and continued. "You know, Mr. Winters, she has a point. I didn't want to increase the dosage, but it might not be a bad idea to have a slight increase in dosage, just to make sure you don't have any lingering issues."

Marcus glared at Elaine, who looked at him supportively. He realized he was just angry and embarrassed about being here. Although she was smothering, he knew she was just concerned.

He conceded Dr. Packard's point and held Elaine's hand reassuringly. "Fine, doc. Whatever you say. When can I be released?"

"Well, I'd like you to consider bed rest for at least twenty-four hours, but you can rest at home."

Marcus nodded, and the doctor left. As he was walking out, Shanice entered. Elaine pulled her hand from his grasp as Shanice grinned. "Aw shit, you're still alive?"

"You seemed surprised."

"Well, I was banking on that insurance policy. My boat needs repairs, so I was kinda holding out in case you croaked, 'cause then I could just buy a new boat."

"Sorry to disappoint, Gib. You still got that boat?"

"I love the Defiant. I'm never giving it up," Shanice said.

The pair laughed, but Marcus knew now wasn't the time. Still, it was just what he needed.

Elaine, however, had had enough. "This is what I'm talking about. You're in the hospital, and instead of taking it easy, you're making jokes about life insurance and new boats."

Before Marcus could respond, Shanice looked at her coldly. "Elaine, get over yourself. Nobody was talking to you."

"Oh no, you don't get to act as if nothing happened. You almost killed him. The doctor said stress management would be helpful, and ever since you showed up in our lives again, you've been nothing but stressful."

"Elaine, calm down," Marcus interjected.

She turned to him in protest. "No, I will not calm down. Not this time. This is your life we're talking about, and I'm the only one who seems to be taking any of this seriously. Tell her she's been nothing but trouble!" she demanded.

Marcus rolled his eyes and shook his head. "Elaine, this is ridiculous. Stop acting li—"

"If you don't tell her how you feel, I will. Shanice, we don't want you in our lives anymore."

Shanice laughed openly, not able to control her response.

Elaine turned to Marcus, who shook his head. "Tell her, Marcus. Tell her we don't want her in our lives."

"Elaine, you're embarrassing yourself."

Her face soured, then turned beet red. She quietly gathered her things. "It's clear I'm not wanted here. Do whatever you want."

Elaine stormed off as Gibson looked at her and then back at Marcus. "Nope, she's not crazy in the least."

"She might be right, Gib."

She turned around and looked back. "So you think this is my fault?"

"I'm not saying that. I don't know what I'm saying."

Marcus sighed as Shanice sat on the rolling chair Elaine had just vacated.

"All right, Marcus, no more of this cat-and-mouse crap. Give me the real."

He looked to the ceiling, closed his eyes, and forced the truth out. "Right before the accident, I was thinking, *what would my life be like if I was Paul Winters?* Paul doesn't have to carry anyone's expectations but his own, and everyone lets him get away with everything. But being born Marcus Bernard Winters II, you spend your life trying to live up to the legend of the great Colonel Marcus Bernard Winters Senior."

Shanice put her hand on his shoulder. "Damn, I didn't know you still felt this way. You've accomplished so much."

"I could become the goddamn president and it would never be enough for the colonel. You know, when I think about it, Gib, I don't even know if joining the military was my idea."

"Now you say that? Going to West Point was all you ever talked about when we were kids."

"When I slow it down and think about it, I didn't really have a choice. It was the only school we ever talked about. I didn't know HBCU's existed, or that there were multiple ways to join the Army. The plan was to graduate from West Point and become a general, but it wasn't my plan. I just knew it would please my dad. Getting into West Point to the officer's academy was his dream for me ever since I could salute, and when I didn't get in, I thought the world had ended. No matter what I did, it could always have been better. Hell, I didn't even know you could join the military as an enlisted person until you told me you were signing up."

"Yeah, I remember you lifted me in the air and spun me around like six times."

"I was so relieved, Gib. I thought, *the dream isn't dead*. I can still serve my country and make him proud. Remember when we had our joint going-away party?

"Yeah."

"Everyone was so supportive and proud and I remember every one of their faces, but the one face that is etched in my brain from that day – crystal clear – is the disappointment in the colonel's eyes. I know that look better than I know any look on the face of this Earth."

Marcus got out of the bed and began to dress himself behind the curtain while Shanice pondered his words.

After a moment she spoke. "Well, it's no secret the colonel has always been tougher on you than Paul. I'll give you that. He's a hard man to please, but he loves you, Marcus."

Marcus pulled back the curtain, now dressed. "Is he proud of me? I've had over 2000 soldiers under my command at any given point, and I didn't lose a single one."

"I know, Marcus. I was there. But what does this have to do with the col—"

"He never even checked on me once I got home. You know, I say I left the military to support Kendra's dreams, and that's mostly true, but I'd be lying if I said I wasn't relieved not to be underneath the man's shadow anymore."

He sat on the edge of the bed and continued his thoughts. "When I lost control of the car, I thought, *maybe this is it. Maybe I'm free of all of it.*"

He looked at Shanice. He could tell his words affected her, and it angered him even more.

"There it is. The disappointment in your eyes says it all. That's how I feel. If it's not you, it's the colonel, Kendra – hell, even Elaine. Everywhere I look, there's just another person disappointed in me."

"Well, obviously God isn't done with you yet. But let me clear something up. I can't speak for anyone else but me, and I know the only reason I was disappointed in you is because from the time we were fourteen years old, you've been the very best person I know. Nobody's come close. Look at all the lives you saved; the lives you're still saving! Even if you left the military for your own reasons doesn't take away the fact that you still uprooted your life for love.

"You took a risk and it didn't work out. But it doesn't define you. You meal-prepped for that woman for six months, jogged every day after your own PT, helped her graduate, helped her get the job. The problem is, you give and you give, to the point where you can't say no to anyone. From my point of view, you are a hero, and always will be one. And I know he has a funny way of showing it, but I know the colonel feels the same way. You gotta talk to your parents, Marcus. You don't want a repeat with things left unresolved. At least let them know what's going on with you."

Marcus put on his shoes and went to the door.

"Yeah, well, I live to fight another day. I'll think about it. Say, why don't we go down to the dock and hop on your boat and spend the rest of the day fishing?"

Shanice shot up out of her seat, surprised by his words. "Are you crazy? You better go check on your woman."

"Elaine is cool, she just—"

"Please, I'm not gonna get between you and that nutjob. Besides, I gotta go to Torres' bachelorette party, so don't tempt me, because I'd love to get out of that."

"Torres is cool. Why don't you want to go?"

"You ever been to a bachelorette party, Winters?" she asked.

The words caught him by surprise. "No, why would I ever go to a bachelorette—"

"Everything is shaped like a dick. The cake is a dick, the cups are dicks, the straws are dicks. Who even makes dick-shaped straws? "

He chuckled at his friend's dilemma. "Okay, rain check then."

"We'll go after you talk to your parents. Deal?"

He examined his friend and thought about her words. "Deal."

14

THE COLONEL

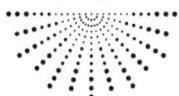

"You're awfully quiet today," Elaine remarked.

Marcus sat quietly on the burgundy loveseat and tapped his fingers, glancing around. He wasn't in the mood to say anything, but he'd committed to Elaine when he found out about his diagnosis. They would have weekly sessions to discuss his feelings about his condition. He'd enjoyed them for a while because they always led to sex. Today he wasn't in the mood for either.

"Marcus."

"Huh?"

"What are you thinking?"

"Nothing, really."

It was partially true; there was one thought on his mind, but he knew it wouldn't be good to bring it up. Tension filled the air.

"Is the new prescription working for you?"

"I haven't crashed into a ditch lately, so I guess so."

"It's bigger than that and you know it."

"Is it though? Look, I haven't had an episode that bad in months. I think part of me thought maybe I was getting better, but it just made me realize I'm not. But nobody ever said life was fair. These are my cards. I just gotta play my hand."

He watched Elaine scribble in her notepad and thought about the absurdity of it all. He was sleeping with her and there was no way she could ever be objective.

"That's understandable, but there's something bothering you."

"I—look, can we cut this session short?"

"We can do that if you can tell me why."

"I mean, look at you. You're giving me real-life therapeutic advice when just an hour ago I was fucking you in the ass. How can I—I don't think it's a good idea for you to be my therapist anymore."

Elaine removed her glasses and leaned over the coffee table. "Marcus, I know we have an unconventional relationship between counselor and patient, but I absolutely can separate our professional relationship from our sexual one."

Marcus pointed towards her cleavage. "See, right there! You leaned over and your nipple slipped out, and now that's all I'm thinking about. You might be able to switch hats, but I don't know if I can."

"What do you mean?"

"I mean, when we're sleeping together, things are great, but the moment you ask me questions of any kind, I get defensive. I feel like I can't really talk to you. Not about this."

"You mean like you can with Gibson?"

"No, I mean, I can't talk to you about this anymore because all you want to do is talk about Gibson."

"Only because she's the source of your erratic behavior."

"What erratic behavior? See, that's what I'm talking about. I haven't done anything that—you know what, screw this. I'm going for a jog. "

Marcus got up and walked into his closet.

As he was changing, Elaine followed him there. "Marcus, you were in the hospital just three days ago. I'm sure Dr. Packard would want you to rest longer than that."

He dismissed her as he continued to find his jogging gear. When he was dressed, he turned to her and said, "Look, either I'm gonna live or I'm gonna die, but what I will not do is sit around here talking through my feelings about death until that day comes. As long as I'm alive, I'm gonna live, so are you coming or not?"

Without a word, Elaine walked into the bathroom and reappeared a few moments later wearing one of her jogging outfits. "You want to do this? Fine. Let's do it."

The pair walked out the door and Marcus put on his headphones.

He was cautious at first, allowing his mind to entertain the idea that he might fall flat on the concrete.

Fuck this. Bravo doesn't quit.

Troubled by his hesitancy, he picked up the pace.

After a few feet, he could hear Elaine's voice over his music.

"Marcus, slow down!"

He ignored her. She had become a constant source of worry and caution, and he wouldn't give in to her request. He needed to prove to himself that this disease would not kill him, not today at least. He was the master of his fate.

He began to sprint, pushing himself harder with each stride, distancing himself from Elaine. When he hit his maximum pace, her voice faded into the background. There would be no more yells of *slow down,* no being treated like he was about to break. No more concern that he was running at full speed.

His heart was pumping faster than ever. If he were to drop dead right now, it would be a happy death.

He ran until he physically could go no further.

He collapsed to the ground, frantically gasping for air. His heartbeat was racing, the reality of his condition – his mortality – setting in.

Just kill me already.

But there was no answer to his plea.

His heart rate slowed and he regained control of his body. No shivering, no shaking – other than from total exhaustion.

He felt fine. He was alive.

He chuckled at the irony of it all as Elaine approached.

She probably felt he was laughing at her expense, but he was too physically and emotionally drained to explain.

"Okay, Marcus, you proved your point. You don't have to laugh at me. Forgive me for giving a damn about you."

He shrugged, unbothered. He didn't want her to give a damn, didn't want this to be happening.

Still, he couldn't let it go. "If you think I was laughing at you, then you don't know me at all."

Elaine walked directly in front of him and quipped, "I know everything about you, Marcus. I know your frustrations, your anxiety, your depression, your anger, and your recklessness, because ever since you got that diagnosis, it's all you ever show me. All I've done is try to be here for you. I've put up with it all; sat silently while your little friends make sly remarks in my face. And I just take it, because I figured maybe you'd see how much I love you. I guess I really am crazy. Despite knowing the worst of you, I still try to believe in the good."

"You're not a victim here, Elaine. You're a volunteer. Leave if I'm too much for you."

He walked away from her and up the driveway towards his home, belatedly noticing a car sitting in front of his house. A car he knew far too well.

"Shit," he cursed.

The smell of freshly-brewed coffee permeated the house, confirming his suspicions.

Marcus rolled his eyes and walked into the kitchen area. An older, well-built, six-foot-four man stood in the kitchen in a perfectly-tailored military uniform, sipping a cup of java and peering out the kitchen window. Marcus released a heavy sigh.

"I see your key still works, Colonel."

"It does, and until you pay me back the down payment for this home, technically, it's my property, too."

"Dad, what are you doing here?"

"Apparently, I'm having shit for coffee. You need to do a better job of cleaning your coffee maker. There are grains in this cup."

Marcus sighed again. His dad was the last person he wanted to see today.

"So, you came all this way to tell me I need to wash dishes better, thanks. Now if you'll excuse me, I'm busy."

As Marcus was about to point his father to the door, Elaine walked in. "Babe, whose car is—Is this your dad? I see the resemblance. So nice to finally meet you. I'm Elaine."

She walked over to shake his hand.

The colonel placed his mug on the bench. "Elaine? Are you in the military?"

"Yes, sir."

"What rank?"

"I'm a corporal, but I should be on track to become sergeant by the end of the year. I served with Marcus in Afghanistan. I served under him, actually, he's a—"

"Then you understand the chain of command."

"Yes, sir, I do."

"Then leave."

He averted his eyes to Marcus, who looked at his father blankly. There was no way to avoid this conversation.

He turned to Elaine, who was turning red.

He gingerly grabbed her hand. "Baby, I need to handle this. I'll talk to you later," he whispered as he kissed her on the cheek.

Elaine nodded somberly and replied, "It's cool. I'll go home and shower. I'll see you later, I guess. It was nice to meet you, Colonel."

"Run along now," the colonel said.

Elaine walked out the door, leaving tension in the air between father and son.

Marcus sat on a barstool. "Well, you came all this way to say something. What is it?"

"She's a downgrade from the last one you were seeing."

"Well, we can't all be so lucky to have as many options as you do, Colonel."

His father ignored his quip and continued. "Talked to Shanice. She's worried about you, and so is your mother."

Marcus covered his face in frustration. "She had no right."

"She had every right. You are my son, and I—"

"Son? That's new, because for as long as I can remember, I've only been a soldier in your little private military."

The colonel took a sip of his coffee. "Let me shed some light for you, since you seem to have forgotten. In this family, I'm the highest-ranking officer. I gave you life, not the other way around, so you show me the respect I deserve."

"Dad, I'm not the one that needs a lecture on family and respect. Your actions are what damn near tore it apart. I'm the one that had to keep your affairs secret since I was twelve. Remember that? So no, I don't feel the need to tell you anything, and I haven't told Mom because she's been through enough already, thanks to you. And as far as my diagnosis goes, I don't need your permission to die. Who I tell is my own damn business."

The colonel smiled and walked over to look Marcus directly in his eyes, forcing Marcus to stand. "I've allowed you a certain courtesy because of your...condition, but if you speak to me like that again in this life – or the next – I'm gonna break off my foot so far up your ass you're gonna shit shoe polish for the rest of your days. Now, are we clear on the level of respect I expect from you?"

Marcus wanted to take a swing at him, but knew that wouldn't end well. Even at his age, he wasn't sure he could best his dad and, despite his condition, he knew his father stood by his words. Respect or fear were the only tools in his parental box.

Marcus gritted his teeth at the helplessness of the situation. "I need some air. Excuse me."

"Sir."

"What?"

"I am the senior officer in this room. The correct phrasing is 'I need some air. Excuse me, sir'."

Marcus scoffed at his father's words and then replied. "Well, I'm leaving, *sir*. You can let yourself out to find better coffee."

15

ALPHA CHARLIE

*S*he's gone too damn far this time.

Marcus murmured to himself as he took a swig of the bottle of tequila he was nursing. He'd spent the last few hours fuming at the conversation with his dad. The more he thought about it, the more upset he became.

His cab was headed toward the military base and the residential homes not too far from the base. He got out and walked toward her condo.

Bang! Bang! Bang! he hit the door furiously. There was no answer.

Bang! Bang! Bang!

Finally, Shanice opened the door. "Marcus? What in the hell is your problem, knocking like the police?"

"You called my dad?" Marcus shouted as he barged into the house.

Shanice closed the door behind him. "Uh, yeah, I called him. What about it?"

"I told you I would handle it!"

"And then you proceeded to not handle it, so I handled it for you."

"What the fuck is wrong with you? You had no right to tell my private business."

"First of all, I told you that you had a finite window to handle it.

Secondly, I seem to remember you telling my aunt Trixie about me trying weed for the first time. I still got a mark on my back be—"

"Here you go again with that story. Look, you shouldn't have been smoking weed at sixteen, and this is totally different!"

"You're right, it's much, much bigger. You are dying!"

"Don't you think I know that?" He paced in front of the door.

Shanice stopped him in his tracks and raised her voice. "No, I don't think you do."

"Trust me, no one, including you, ever misses an opportunity to remind me."

"Then why are you shutting everyone out? You're being reckless, Marcus. Look at you, you're drunk right now."

"Don't get all high and mighty with me, Shanice. Elaine was right. Ever since you came back into my life, it's been nothing but trouble."

"Oh, you're putting that on me now?"

"Where else should I put it, Gib?"

"I want you to blame the guy who left a bar drunk, fully knowing he could lose control of a car. If I knew things were that bad, I would've never let you drive. And now you're drunk again?

"Look, Marcus, I have been trying to let you work through whatever it is you're feeling, but all I see is you working through a bottle of tequila."

Marcus took out one of many bottles of meds and lifted it in the air.

"You don't have to worry about me losing control of anything, because they pump me so full of this shit, all I can do is concentrate."

He took the pill bottle and threw it against the wall, pills flying everywhere.

He started towards the door but quickly backtracked. "Just to be clear on my reckless behavior, I want to point out that *you* started not only that first bar fight, but the second bar fight that got my black ass thrown in jail, and I said nothing at all about it. All I did was have your back, like always."

Shanice drew closer. "You had my back? You didn't bother telling me the truth about Kendra, let alone tell me how you're feeling about—"

"What? Dying?"

"Yes, motherfucker, dying! The same shit we talked about in dozens of foxholes. Do you know how many times we talked about death before we went on missions where we thought we might not make it back? Because I've lost count. The same way you came to me when you found out you didn't get into West Point, you should have come to me now. I would have had your back like I always do."

"What do you want me to do, Gib?"

"I want you to talk, Marcus! If not to me, then to the colonel, or Hayes, or even Elaine. Hell, anyone is better than no one, because you are not handling this well."

Marcus pounded on the door in frustration. "I don't want you to give a damn! I don't want Elaine to give a damn, and I don't want my pops to give a damn!"

"Then what in the hell do you want, Marcus?"

"I want Kendra to give a damn! Okay?"

He screamed as he punched the door.

He began to weep openly, and Shanice ran over to catch him as he fell into her arms, sobbing uncontrollably.

He was naked in his honesty.

Shanice hugged him as he continued. "She just left me, Gib. Why'd she do that?"

He sobbed as Shanice held him.

It wasn't true. He knew it. He didn't even mean it.

Everything was his fault, but in this moment, he wanted to live in a world where what he wanted mattered, and right now, all he wanted was to be with Kendra.

He sobbed and continued, "You know, now and then, I can't help but wonder how I got this disease. Maybe I was infected with some nerve agent while we were overseas. I'm a guinea pig for one of those injections the military gave us. But then I think maybe this is my punishment for what I did to Kendra. Maybe this is my karma. All those times we cheated death overseas and I come home for it to end like this? I fucked up, Gib, I'm dying and I'm still fucking up. I can live with all my mistakes, but I can't die knowing that she thinks I don't love her, because I do."

"Then stop being a jackass and tell her. Tell her everything. Maybe not all at once, but tell her how you feel. Remember, you're in her heart too, and that shit doesn't go away easily. She'll listen to you."

"You think so?" he asked as she rubbed the back of his head.

"I know so. What's not to like about you? You're smart, driven, and while sometimes you're as dumb as a bag of dicks, I think that anyone who really knows you, knows that you mean well."

Marcus looked into her eyes. She wiped his remaining tears as her words comforted him.

"Thank you."

"No problem."

"No, I mean it. You've always been there for me, Gib. You've always been there to pick me up when I've been down. I love you for that."

"That's what friends are for," she replied.

Her eyes softened, and he thought he caught something in her gaze. Something sensual, comforting, deeper than how a friend would look at him.

He acted on his urge to kiss her, abandoning the well-established boundaries of their friendship.

He felt her startle and pull away.

"Marcus, what are you doing?" She asked, shocked.

He immediately realized his mistake.

Embarrassed, he replied, "I'm...sorry. I should go."

He tried to walk around her, but she stood in his way.

He stepped in the opposite direction, only to be met by her again.

He peered into her eyes. The softness from earlier had been replaced with a lustful fire.

Shanice pulled him in and kissed him passionately.

Her passion was met with his own.

A firestorm of intensity erupted as he lifted her up and walked her into her bedroom. They undressed each other feverishly, their chemistry growing into a raging inferno.

He tossed her now-naked body onto the bed and began to run his tongue alongside her neck down to her beautiful bouncing breasts, settling his lips on her left nipple as he bit down sharply.

She welcomed his aggressive nature and returned the favor by sinking her teeth deep into his shoulder. He moved his tongue over to the other nipple and applied the same pleasure.

"Oh damn," she moaned in ecstasy.

Marcus climbed on top of her, looking into her eyes for what seemed like the first time. He wanted her, but he knew what this meant. "If we do this, we can nev— "

"Shhh… I want you," she whispered.

He nodded in agreement and entered her, her heat and moisture overwhelming him.

"Oh, shit," he moaned as he continued to slide into her wet, pulsating pussy. He watched her eyes widen. A slight gasp of pleasure followed.

"Give me more," she demanded.

She pulled him in and began kissing him passionately as he pumped his long, dense, throbbing dick into the core of her. With each stroke, he became more comfortable with what they had committed to.

It wasn't the kinky or aggressive sex he had with Elaine, or the tender lovemaking he'd had with Kendra. He'd never experienced this feeling before. A lifetime connection was being explored intimately. The friend who knew everything about him explored him with a familiarity he desperately desired. They had crossed a line they could never come back from, and happily so.

Her body lent itself to a language they were creating. As they rolled over, she climbed on top of his throbbing dick and rocked gracefully, eventually picking up pace, never breaking eye contact.

"Cum inside of me," she whispered.

He thrust harder, faster, and deeper than before. He released his seed in between the sweetness of her walls and moaned savagely.

She climaxed on top of him and he rolled over, locking eyes with her. Exhausted by the experience.

"You're so beautiful," he said, stroking her cheek as he began fading into sleep.

"Hold me," she said. She slid underneath him and the pair fell into a deep, intimate slumber.

16

CHARLIE FOXTROT

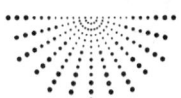

*W*here *am I?* Marcus thought to himself.

He glanced around the room and saw Mr. Elephant – a stuffed animal Shanice had had since she was four.

Aw shit.

He'd been drunk around Shanice too many times to count, and in all those instances, not once did it involve him pulling his dick out. In fact, he couldn't recall ever being remotely attracted to her.

Come on, Marcus. Shanice?

He tried to convince himself that maybe it didn't happen, but as memories from the night before came flooding back, he knew it wasn't true.

Gibson was the one friendship he never wanted to ruin. She was like a sister to him, until she wasn't.

What bothered him the most was the fact that thinking about the events of last night didn't bother him at all.

"Damn it, Marcus!" he muttered to himself. Disappointed in his feelings.

He knew he'd been drunk, but as he recalled looking into her eyes the night before, it didn't matter. Nothing mattered but being next to her.

He turned toward her. She was still asleep.

He stared at her sleeping peacefully.

She's still out. Maybe I should leave.

He was looking around for his clothing when he heard her voice.

"Morning."

He looked over at her. She was just as beautiful as she was last night.

"Hey," he replied, unsure of what to say.

He turned in bed to face her. He wanted to kiss her but wasn't sure if it was what she wanted.

This unfamiliar territory thoroughly confused Marcus. He decided to break the ice.

"Look, Shanice... I just wanted to sa—"

"Marcus, we're adults. It happened. You were drunk, I was drinking before you got here, and I haven't had any in a while. So we sport fucked."

Her response was disappointing. Perhaps a small part of him wanted this to be more.

He nodded. "Yeah, I was dru—wait, what? We sport fucked?"

Shanice sat up in the bed and tossed Marcus his underwear and shirt.

"Yeah, you were crying, boo-hooing and shit, and I'm like *the guy's about to die. Let me just give him some pussy so he'll shut up.*"

Marcus smiled at her statement. Apparently he was the only one dealing with these new feelings, so he dismissed them for now.

"Well, I guess that means things are good between us."

"Always, Winters, but now you gotta go."

"Damn, it's like that?"

"I got shit to do," she said as she threw his shirt at him.

The pair got dressed and Marcus walked out of the bedroom, looking back as Shanice put on black spandex pants.

Damn, Gib got a fat ass.

He fought the urge to walk over to her and instead said, "At least tell me... was it good?"

"I'm not telling you shit, because that would mean we plan on doing it again, which we don't, so let's move on before this gets anymore weird."

"Same old, Gib. Fair point." He nodded in agreement and opened the bedroom door.

Although he didn't want to put it behind him, he knew it would only make his already-complex life more troublesome, so he let it go.

Before he walked out the door, he turned to her and said, " Wanna meet for a drink later and go over next week's plans?"

"Marcus, you realize that drinking is how all this happened in the first place, right?" She shook her head in exasperation. "I think I'm gonna go out on the boat later. What you need to do is go home and call your parents and have an honest conversation."

Reality came crashing back to him.

He stopped in his tracks and stared at the front door.

Shanice walked over to him as he stood in silence.

"I don't want to die, Gib."

"I know."

"I'm just figuring it all out. My lane in life, my calling... I want to see it through."

"I know."

Shanice hugged him and he softened against her.

After a spell, she kissed him on the cheek. "When I first got here from Nevis, I thought I had it all figured it out, and when the culture shock of the fast-paced city hit me, I was overwhelmed, homesick and I didn't have any friends. My family's expectations were on my shoulders, and I wanted to go home. One day I met this ninth-grader, wise beyond his years, who told me, 'We can't control the hand we're given. We can only control how we play it.'"

Marcus grinned. "You remember that?"

"Go home, Marcus."

The two shared one last embrace, and Marcus walked out the door.

He knew she was right. It didn't matter how much time he had left; it was what he did with the time that counted.

As he walked out of the house, he looked at his phone.

Missed calls Elaine (28)

Marcus booked a car service then scrolled through his contacts. After two rings, the phone picked up.

"What do you want, asshole?"

"Yo, Hayes. What are you doin'?"

"In the garage cleaning guns."

"Again?"

"If you stay ready, you don't have to get ready."

"Need any help?"

"I think I got a bottle around here. We could split it while we work."

"Cool, I'm on the way."

He hung up the phone. He'd never needed an invitation to Hayes' house. He was always either cleaning his guns or drinking, and right now he'd be happy doing either, anything to get his mind off what he wanted to say to Elaine.

It wasn't long before he was pulling into Ryan's driveway. As he walked up, Ryan tossed him a Bud Light can, which he promptly opened and chugged.

The smell of gun oil permeated the garage. Marcus walked up to see Hayes reassembling his Glock 9 mm pistol. Without a word, Marcus found a gun still assembled, picked it up, and sat on the workbench next to Hayes. The two worked in silence until four of the guns were cleaned.

"I don't know why cleaning guns is so relaxing. Must have something to do with all that military training," Marcus said.

"Well, a gun is simple, Winters, and soldiers are simple folk. You give us a task. We execute orders. If only life were that easy."

Ryan finished his last weapon and threw his empty beer can into a trash can. He walked over to a makeshift cabinet and pulled out a bottle of Crown Royal Reserve, taking a sip before handing the bottle over to Marcus, who took a swig as well.

"What's on your mind, Winters?"

Marcus took a sip out of the bottle and handed it back. "Just thinking about how far we've come, the two of us. Hell, we couldn't stand each other overseas. Now we're business partners."

"Funny how life works out, right?" Hayes said as they passed the bottle back and forth.

"The night Jackson died, and we got locked up, why did you tell General Reese that I was the guy for the job? I mean, you know I'm sick. You could have just as easily said it was your idea. Hell, I half expected you to do just that."

"You think that little of me, huh?"

"No, I just remember the Ryan Hayes that would take advantage of every opportunity to claim credit for good ideas."

"Well, it's not really fair to judge a man on his past, is it?"

Marcus nodded, conceding his point.

Ryan took a sip of the whiskey and leaned on the table. "You know, the one thing I learned in the military is, if two people are in charge at the same time, everyone is gonna die. Now, you can never repeat this, because I'll deny it to the grave, but when we were overseas, I realized you were a better leader than me. I was so focused on kicking your ass, proving I was the best, that it consumed me. That's what got my men killed.

"You, on the other hand, were focused on the mission, a consummate professional. You made it your personal responsibility to make sure everyone – including me – got back stateside. Brainstorming in that cell with you and Gibson that night, it was an easy choice. If Brothers in Arms was going to be a thing, you were going to be its face and leader."

Marcus sipped the whiskey and fought back the onslaught of emotions. Ryan had turned out to be much more than a rival, more than a friend. He truly was a brother.

He handed the whiskey back to Hayes. "Had to be a tough choice."

"Don't get me wrong, the old me would've kicked my ass. He would've hated this idea so much, but this is about the soldiers. It's the right call."

"Look, Winters, we're all a little fucked up. Every single person on this goddamn rock has a problem, and we're all gonna die. We're just bargaining for time. For you to take your last days and dedicate it to this organization? That takes not only balls, but selflessness that I don't think another man on base has. Helping these vets is the best service I've ever done for this country, for my fellow man. As good guys go, you're one of the best men I've ever met. I know it, Gibson knows, Elaine knows it, and even though Kendra is down in Houston probably getting plowed by a Texas-sized di—"

"Hayes!"

"My bad, you know I'm a straight-shooter. Point is, she knows it, too. You're a hell of a soldier, Winters, and a hell of man. Anyone who wants to judge you for your past mistakes needs to bring a mirror to judge their own."

Marcus sat there in silence for a while, contemplating Hayes' words and his actions over the past twenty-four hours.

"Yeah, but all my mistakes aren't in the past. I slept with Gib."

Ryan's eyes grew wide as he slammed his hand on the table. "Son of a bitch! I knew it."

"Wait, what? How did you know?"

"You know, Winters, you're a smart guy, but Gibson is right: when it comes to women, you really are as dumb as a bag of dicks." Hayes chuckled. "Besides, the two of you always had chemistry."

"It's a line I never wanted to cross, man. I'm not sure what could make matters worse. I stayed out all night. Now I gotta go explain it to Elaine."

"Well, as far as you and Gib go, she's a big girl. She knows what she wants, so I'm not worried about you on that front. But with Holt, you gotta use that time-honored military tradition."

"Which is?"

"Lie."

Marcus chuckled. "I'm done lying, man. I just want to live in peace, and own my mistakes at this point. Thing is, ever since it happened with Gib, I can't stop thinking about her. Still, I just feel like I owe Elaine an explanation."

Ryan took another swig of the bottle and then turned to Marcus and, in a more direct tone, said, "You're dying, Winters. You don't owe anyone a damn thing. Now if you want to bang Gibson, I say go for it. If you want a threesome with Gibson and Holt at the same time, I only ask that you let me hold the camera. But if you want to be the guy that I would follow into hell, the guy that you keep running from, then pull yourself up by the jockstrap and be accountable. No more of this pussyfooting around shit. Take your lumps and eat your vegetables. Because the soldiers that are coming to us, they need that guy to lead them. That guy was why Bravo company never quit, never failed. They fought, and they fought like hell. Whatever you choose, I'm here for you, brother."

The words comforted Marcus.

He stood up and dusted his hands off before shaking Ryan's hand. "I'm out, brother. Thank you."

Marcus left his friend and headed back home, mulling Ryan's words over in his head.

As he pondered, he replayed his night of passion with Shanice. The beautiful, gentle nature in which they touched. The way their eyes connected in the pale moonlight and the harrowing way they climaxed while staring into each other's eyes.

He thought about the fullness of her lips and the moisture of her thighs. He thought about how natural it felt, and he yearned to go back to her place instead of home.

She was his best friend, after all. In fact, the only reason there had been any distance between them lately was because of how threatened Kendra was about their friendship.

His emotions and memories were building to one inescapable question:

Hold up... do I... am I... in love with Shanice?

"No! Hell no," he said aloud, drawing a concerned look from the cab driver.

Dismissing the thought as quickly as it came, he chuckled as they pulled into his driveway.

Elaine's car was sitting next to his.

"Shit."

He paid the driver and got out of the cab, headed inside.

When he entered, he could smell the scent of lavender incense filling the home. He knew that meant that Elaine had been smoking a joint, which meant she was upset.

Here we go.

Elaine was sitting on the cream loveseat sipping a glass of red wine, and there was an ashtray on the glass coffee table. He looked at the contents of the ashtray and found two marijuana cigarettes.

Yep, she's pissed.

He watched her in silence. Her face was red, and her eyes were puffy. It was clear she'd been crying.

He sat on the seat next to her as she sipped her wine.

"Where were you?"

His instinct was to lie. Marcus knew Hayes would vouch for him, but he was tired of lying. He was dying. There was no need to.

"I was at Gibson's," he replied.

Elaine chuckled sardonically, taking another sip of the wine. "Did you sleep with her?"

"I did."

She put the glass of wine down and hung her head. He watched her process his words.

A tear fell from her eye when she asked, "Is it out of your system?"

"I'm... not sure."

Elaine sipped from the glass and put it down. She stood up and walked into the bedroom, returning after a minute with a full duffle bag.

"Elaine, wait, I—"

"Marcus, I've done everything I possibly could. I've been here for you, tried to help you get healthy. I've let you fuck me in every way imaginable. I've cooked, I've cleaned, I've done everything. But you know what I realized? No one appreciates it. I shouldn't have to list the things I've done for you. If you can't see what I've done, that I'm in your corner – that I'm the kind of woman who will be here for you always – then maybe this wasn't meant to be. With whatever time you have left, I want you to find what makes you happy. And I need to be doing the same. We both deserve that. I'm tired of trying to please you, and constantly coming up short. You know who and what I am, good and bad."

"Elaine, I—"

"I'm not finished! Despite what everyone thinks, I've shown you respect, support, submission, and loyalty. No one – not even you – can argue with that. So now the only question is, do you want to be with me? I've made it known how I feel, and I don't want to come in second place anymore. Not to Kendra, not to Gibson. Not to anyone. I want to be yours and I don't want to share."

He felt the weight of her words in a way he wasn't expecting. For the first time, he wasn't seeing Elaine as just a babbling, neurotic therapist, or some side-piece. She was a woman, and he'd hurt her with his own selfish needs. He didn't want to be that man anymore.

Before he could respond, she walked over to him and hugged him.

"I won't even make it hard. Call me if I'm ever enough."

She kissed him one last time and walked out of the door.

17

TWO KLICKS IN THE WRONG DIRECTION

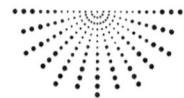

What about your friends?

*W*hat the hell have I done?

Shanice had been replaying that same thought ever since Marcus had left this morning. As she straightened up her home, she couldn't get the thought out of her head.

"Marcus. I fucked Marcus fucking Winters," she repeated over and over.

Shanice had never had a problem with confidence, except for now, with her best friend.

There was only one person she could talk to about this, since Marcus was obviously a no-go. She picked up the phone and found the contact. After a few rings, they picked up.

"Hello?"

"Hey, Trina."

"What's up, Shan? What you doin'?"

"I… I'm not even sure how to say it."

"Something wrong?"

"No, it's just…" Shanice paused.

"Shanice… are you okay?"

"I'm fine, it's…"

"Just spit it out."

"I slept with Marcus."

There was no response. Shanice looked at the phone to see if her signal had dropped. She put the phone on speaker.

"Trina. Are you there?"

"I'm here."

"Did you hear what I said?"

"Mmmm hmm"

"So… what do you have to say?"

"Girl, bye."

"Trina."

"Look, I've just done two surgeries back-to-back, and I'm still trying to get off work to get ready for my dick appointment, so I ain't got time for you to be playing on my phone."

"Trina, please, I'm serious. It ha—"

"What do you want me to say to you, Shan? You've been running behind that boy since the ninth grade. I ain't got time for this foolish—"

"Trina, I really need to talk about it, please."

Trina paused before replying. "Damn it, girl, hold on, let me clear my other line."

There was a silent pause.

"Mama. I'm gonna call you back. Shanice just got some dingaling to knock the cobwebs off her coo—"

"It's still me, Trina."

"Shanice?"

"Yes."

"Oh, my bad, Mama must've hung up. Finish what you were saying."

She scoffed at her friend's nonchalance and continued. "Well, like I was saying, he came over last night and one thing led to another."

"You know what? Let's make this quick. You boned him. Was it good?"

"It was… amazing."

"Did you shave?"

"It wasn't like that. Why are yo—"

"Shan, we're gonna do this my way or I'm hanging up. Now, did you shave?"

Now concerned, Shanice pulled on her spandex pants and looked down.

"I'm in the danger zone, but we're good."

"Okay, did you give him some again this morning?"

"Trina, I—"

"Look, Shanice, respectfully, I'm not gonna sit here and relive how you've been sniffing behind this boy your whole life. Let's just get right to the point."

"Trina, that's some bullshit and you know it."

"Oh, please! Tell it to somebody who wasn't there. When you first got here to live with your aunt, the first week at Lee High you saw that boy and you been drooling behind him ever since, and instead of telling him how you felt, you played the homie, lover, friend role, 'cept all he saw was the homie and friend part."

"And that's how I accidentally fell into the friendzone."

"And been digging a deeper hole ever since."

Shanice plopped down on the couch and rubbed her face. "That was a long time ago. I've—"

"Okay, let's keep playing stupid," Trina interrupted.

Shanice rolled her eyes as Trina continued.

"Exhibit B. When we got out of high school and you both went into the military, I thought, *great, she's gonna finally tell him how she feels and get her back blown out, and they're gonna be booty-battle-buddies* but when you got back home and I asked you about it, what did you say?"

"I told you how he met Kendra and I supported him."

"And so, he took your advice, because that's what any friend would do. Except now, you were sick to your stomach, calling me and telling me how he could do better."

"But that was a long time ago, too. I've dated – hell, I was with Rodney, and we had a good relationship. I moved past those feelings a long time ago, T."

"Girl, now, we both know Rodney was there to feed you when you were hungry and eat you when you're horny."

"Then he stopped doing that. But the point is, I was over Marcus."

"So, if you really feel that you've moved past him, tell me, why did you let last night happen?"

Shanice went silent. She knew it was pointless. For all her faults, Trina was always a straight-shooter, and was the only person besides Marcus she could be honest with.

She let out a deep sigh and replied. "I don't know, T. He was down, I've never seen him like that, not even when he didn't get into West Point. I just wanted to be there for him."

"Did you or your kitty cat want to be there for him?"

"What? What's that supp—"

"Girl, lie to your momma, lie to Marcus, hell, even lie to yourself. But don't lie to me. I know two things: one, you've been in love with that boy since the ninth grade. And two, the only reason you didn't give it up to him on the night he didn't get into West Point is 'cause your aunt was there to cockblock. You've been rubbing on your kitty cat for so long I'm surprised your clit doesn't have a permanent thumbprint on it. Like it or not, last night was inevitable."

It was the hard truth she'd been avoiding.

She shook her head in disbelief and said, "I can't believe this shit. After all these years, I still love him."

"Ding, ding, ding! Now, get off my phone and go tell him what you should've told him years ago."

"Girl, how am I supposed to tell Marcus any of that now? He just told me he misses his ex, not to mention he's dating this crazy-ass white girl."

"Hold up, Marcus is dating a white girl?"

"Tee, I—"

"So, you mean to tell me you got competition with Kendra… and Karen?" Trina belted into laughter as Shanice rolled her eyes.

Finally, she cut her friends' laughter short. "Ha, ha, ha, hoe. Now can you please tell me what I should do?"

"What do you want me to tell you, Shan? You've always liked him, but you never wanted to cross some imaginary line in your head, and every time he comes to you with a problem, instead of telling him how you feel you give him friendly advice and that's… say it with me."

"How I ended up in the friendzone. I know, I know."

"Girl, y'all exhausting."

"Trina—"

"I'm serious. I can't deal with no man where dick ain't at least on the discussion table. All the problems, but none of the pipe? What's the point?"

"Believe it or not, Trina, not everyone thinks about sex like that—"

"We're not talking about everyone, we're talking about you. While you were overseas risking your life, instead of being a supportive friend, telling him how much you admired him, you should've been getting his missile ready for launch. Now he's out here being Black Army Ken for White Army Barbie and you're on the phone cock-blocking me from a whole 'nother state. I'm just saying, you can keep playing these games if you want to, but eventually he's going to marry one of these women and you're gonna be looking like Sanaa Lathan in *The Best Man* sitting next to Queen Latifah talking about 'when did you fall in love with hip hop'?"

"I'm pretty sure that's the storyline to *Brown Sugar*, not—"

"Bitch! The point is, it'll be the plotline to Shanice Gibson's life if you don't open your mouth and tell him how you feel!"

Shanice sighed and closed her eyes.

Trina was right, and she knew it. She just didn't want to admit it to herself.

She hung her head in frustration and said, "Story of my incredibly stupid life. The man I fell in love with in high school has got six months left to live and wishes he could spend that six months with someone else. Cupid can go suck a giant, uncircumcised dick."

"Come again?"

Shanice paused, realizing she'd not told Trina about Marcus's condition. She quickly tried to change the subject. "Nothing, I—"

"Oh, it's too late now, Shan Shan. If you don't tell me what you just said, I'm gonna find Marcus on social media and tell him you've been trying to get him to do all those pushups on top of you since you had braces."

"Trina, I will break your clavicle. Don't play with me."

"I said what I said. You know I'll do it because light-skinned Jermaine still be around here trying to get your number from me. Now spill. The. Tea."

Shanice sighed and relented to her friend's threat. "Okay, look girl, this has to stay between you and me."

"Girl, who am I gonna tell? The only officer I know is Colonel Sanders. Quit stalling and spit it out."

"You cannot repeat this. Marcus doesn't have long to live. He didn't even tell his parents about it, which is how all this got started in the first place."

"Shanice... girl, I'm sorry. What does he have?"

"Some kind of advanced Parkinson's disease that makes him have seizures and convulsions."

"Damn... I'm sorry, Shan."

"Yeah, the doctor on the base gave him a year to live about six months ago. He takes a ton of medication to control his symptoms."

There was silence in the air. After a while, Trina broke it. "Shanice, I'm sorry. All joking aside, I know how much you care for him. Which is why you gotta tell him how you really feel, before it's too late."

"You're right. I know. I told him that last night was a mercy fuck."

"You told him that?"

"Yeah."

"You are too smart to be this stupid."

"Trina—"

"Girl, go tell that man the truth. Not tomorrow, not at his funeral, today."

"Fine. I was gonna go out on the boat, but he threw his pills all over the place, so as soon as I pick them up I'll go over to his place and maybe we'll have a talk."

"What is he taking?" Trina asked.

Shanice picked up the bottle and read the prescription. "Something called... Haldol."

"Impossible."

"Trina, I'm looking at the bottle in my hand."

"Are you sure he was diagnosed with Parkinson's?"

"Yes, girl, he is. I know that for a fact."

"Then there's no reason he should be taking Haldol."

"What? What are you talking about?"

"Shan, let's not forget, I'm a whole medical doctor in these streets. Haldol is an older antipsychotic medication that actually induces muscle spasms. It has the opposite side effect of what someone with Parkinson's should be taking. Any first year resident would know that. You sure he's not having hallucinations or is a stroke survivor? Other than the stroke he was putting between your legs, I mean."

"You are such an ass, you know that? No, I'm certain it's some aggressive form of Parkinson's. I remember that clearly."

"Do you know what other medication he's on?"

Shanice put the keys to her boat in her pocket and slipped on her tennis shoes. "No, but I'm about to find out. I'll call you back later, girl."

She walked out the door, not yet sure what to do with the information, but she knew where to start.

18

BRAVO NEVER FAILS

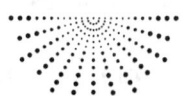

"*And* while tropical storm Susan wasn't supposed to make landfall in the vicinity, new projections show the storm has altered co—"

Click.

Shanice turned off the radio as she drove over to the base. She wanted answers, and Dr. Packard was the only person who could give them to her. As she pulled up to the gate, she was met by one of the military police, who stopped her car.

She opened the window.

"What's going on?"

"Storm's coming in pretty heavy. We're shutting the base down early, giving everyone time to shelter in place."

The base being empty gave her the perfect opportunity to talk to Dr. Packard, provided he hadn't left yet.

She looked back at the soldier. "I won't be long, just gotta grab a few things."

"Yes, ma'am." The soldier nodded and let her onto the base.

As she parked her car, she got a text from Marcus.

Hey, can we talk?

She examined the text, not sure how to respond. A few moments later, she replied.

I'd like that. I can't right now, on the verge of some important news, but I'll tell you about it later.

She hit send and got out of the car. She walked to the VA wing where Dr. Packard worked, only to be met with silence. It was already cleared out.

"Shit."

He must have left already.

As she turned around to continue her search, she heard her name.

"Sergeant Gibson, you're still here? I thought they evacuated the base for the storm?"

"Dr. Packard, you're… yeah, it was, but I've been having this nagging issue with my shoulder. I was wondering if you could look at it."

"Sergeant, I'd love to, but this storm is approaching. If you make an appointment I'll—"

"It will only take a second, Doctor."

She could tell he was apprehensive, but based on her previous experiences with him, he'd always been a nervous man.

The doctor nodded as Shanice sat on the medical bench for him to inspect her shoulder. She scanned the room as he picked up his clipboard and walked over to examine her.

"What seems to be troubling you?"

"Well, it seems like I have been having issues with my muscles locking up on me from time to time. I was hoping you'd be able to prescribe me something for that."

"Well, without the necessary blood work or anything more detailed, I can't hand out a prescription, Sergeant."

"Come on, Doc," she pleaded as she hopped off the bench and walked around. "Can't you just give me some of those pills you gave Sergeant Winters? It seems to work great for him."

The doctor put down his clipboard. "Sergeant Gibson, his condition is an extreme case. Besides, I don't think what you have would require that kind of medication. Now, if you'll excuse me—"

"What did you prescribe him?"

"Excuse me?"

"You know, the meds. What did you give him?"

"Sergeant, that's confidential information. I can't divulge what a patient is taking. Even with his authorization, that's not the recommended best practice."

"Then I'll look for myself."

Shanice walked over to the medical files, Dr. Packard attempting to block her.

"I can't let you do that."

"Doctor, if you don't get out of my way, we're gonna see how well you can write prescriptions with two broken hands."

Dr. Packard shook his head in defeat and stood to the side.

Shanice opened the files and searched for *Winters, M.*

Once she found it, she became engrossed in the notes.

Bumex and Diuril have properties that dehydrate the body, resulting in severe muscle spasms. Combined with any other mood stabilizer, except for Haldol, this is acceptable. But if you are on Haldol, it has the involuntary effect of weight loss, insomnia, depression, and seizures.

"Okay, Doc, none of these indicate Marcus has any medical condition whatsoever. What the hell is going on here?" she said as she continued to read the notes.

There was no response.

"Doc, explain to me what the hell is going on, or I'm going to talk with the general to find out wh—"

"Actually, I might be able to help you with that."

Shanice turned around at the familiar voice, only to be met with a cloud of white dust, momentarily blinding her.

"What the hell?" she exclaimed.

She tried to make out her assailant but before she could, an overpowering sensation took over her body. She lost control of her limbs and collapsed onto the ground. She was paralyzed and losing consciousness fast.

Shanice tried to lift her head, but the paralytic agent was now in her bloodstream. She was at the mercy of her attacker.

As she began to pass out, the assailant's face slowly came into focus. There was no question who it was.

"*Elaine.*"

BRAVO NEVER QUITS

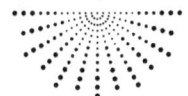

The Storm Part II

"*R*ise and shine, Gibson!"

Shanice heard Elaine's voice as she fought through the grogginess of the drug.

Her head was throbbing, and her vision was blurry, but none of that concerned. She still couldn't move. The drug she'd been dosed with still paralyzed her body.

She groaned.

Although she was immobile, she could feel every sensation in body, most of which were painful. Droplets of water covered her forehead and found their way into the bleeding wound at the corner of her lip.

She could smell the ocean in between each breath. A crackle of thunder roared against the melody of crashing waves.

She looked around and instantly recognized her second home: her boat, The Defiant. Elaine and Dr. Packard were both standing on the deck wearing green Army ponchos to cover themselves from the increasing torrent of rain.

As Elaine walked over, a clap of thunder and lightning clashed above the clouds in the night's sky.

"So, tell me... how was your nap?"

She kicked Shanice violently in the ribcage, forcing her to grunt in pain.

Shanice tried to stand but to no avail. The drugs were still very heavy in her system and she couldn't do anything to defend herself. She could feel Elaine's malevolent nature even above the power of the waves that were rocking the boat.

Elaine looked at her and chuckled. "Yeah, you won't be able to move anytime soon. The stuff I dosed you with was pretty powerful. Besides, this makes for a much more pleasant conversation, and we're overdue for some girl-time, don't you think?"

"What did you do to me, you crazy, white bitch?" Shanice huffed.

Elaine chuckled and kicked her again.

This time Shanice heard a crunch.

Although she couldn't move, she could feel everything, and she knew Elaine had definitely broken a rib.

Shanice suppressed her yelps of pain in between the chorus of the thunder. She refused to give Elaine the pleasure of knowing she was hurt.

Elaine walked over and sat down on a crate next to Shanice, pushing back the hood of the trench coat.

"I just gave you something to relax. I mean, it's not my lover's cock, but I think it will do, don't you?" she said as she pressed her foot against Shanice's neck, cutting off her airway.

After a spell, she lifted her foot.

As Shanice gasped for air, she tried to wiggle her toes. Some sensation was returning, but not enough to fight back.

Okay, Gib, whatever's in your system, you gotta hope adrenaline can compensate for it. Play it smart. Provoke her, just keep her talking, and pray that the adrenaline will override whatever's in your system. It's your only chance.

She glanced toward the edge of the boat where she was lying, looking for the flare gun that Elaine knew nothing about.

I just have to keep her talking until I get enough strength to get to the gun.

She looked back at Elaine and shouted, "Your lover's dick."

"Excuse me?"

"Well, you said 'cock' before. I'm correcting you. It's your lover's 'dick'."

"Are you fucking serious right now?"

"I'm just saying, if you're gonna kill me to be with a black man, at least know that never in the history of his blackness has he called it a cock. He calls it a dick."

"And just how in the hell do you know that?"

"'Cause like you said, I fucked him."

Wham.

Elaine kicked her in the ribs again, much harder than before. Shanice could feel the pain of a second rib breaking. She wheezed in pain, but with each breath came the hope that her body would fight the drugs in her system to help her defend herself.

"You're poisoning him, Elaine, and I'm not sure what you have on the doc, but I know none of it's going to work."

Elaine yelled back, completely unhinged. "I am helping him! Because despite what everyone thinks, us being together is the best thing for him. I will not be Matthew Robinson!"

Puzzled by the statement, Shanice asked, "Do you hear yourself right now? Who the fuck is Matthew Robinson?"

A clash of thunder roared out as Elaine responded.

"Matthew Robinson was a world-class athlete who absolutely destroyed the Olympic Record at the Berlin Games in 1936, only to come in second to Jesse Owens. Owens went on to become a legend, while Matthew lived out his days being a janitor at a white-only middle school in Pasadena. Do you know the difference in their finish times?"

"No, sorry, I'm not up to speed on crazy-bitch trivia," Shanice responded.

Elaine kicked her in the ribs again.

113

Shanice clenched her eyes in pain and forced herself to wiggle her toes as Elaine continued.

"Four-tenths of a second, smartass. I mean, it hardly seems fair. But to further add insult to injury, Matthew Robinson had a little brother who was also an athlete. His name was Jackie, who also became a legend.

"Every time I find a sliver of happiness, there you are, like the little whore you are, just waiting to steal everything I care about. *Not this time*, I told myself after the General's Games. I will never be Matthew Robinson."

As she continued rambling, Shanice tested her limbs to see if her senses had returned.

Just keep her talking.

Shanice could feel her extremities, she just needed full control of her legs.

She looked to her captor. "Elaine, I don't know shit about the Robinson family or the Olympics, but I do know you're one sick puppy that's poisoning a man she says she loves. I'm not sure what you've got on the doctor, or why he's helping you, but I'm gonna tell you this right now: it's never going to work, because the truth of the matter is, you could never be Matthew Robinson. Because he had talent. From what I hear on base, your only talent is putting a dick – excuse me, a cock – in your mouth and blowing it."

"Shut up!" Elaine barked as she kicked her in the ribs again.

The adrenaline was finally surging through her body. She could feel her feet again.

Good girl, Gib.

She turned to Dr. Packard, who had been standing idly by.

"Doc, are you just gonna stand there while she throws your entire career away? This crazy bitch is standing in a trench coat in the middle of a tropical storm talking about Jackie Robinson's brother. Does that sound like something a sane person would be doing?"

"I said, shut up!" Elaine tried to kick her again.

This time Shanice blocked her ribs from the impact. She managed to grab Elaine's foot, causing her to fall.

Despite being still heavily drugged, she was able to stand.

Elaine climbed to her feet as well.

"No!" Elaine shouted. "Stupid Elaine! Stupid, stupid, stupid!"

The crackle of thunder roared in the night as Gibson took a defensive stance.

SHANICE WAS in no condition to fight Elaine, but Elaine didn't know that. She knew if she got to the flare gun, she could defend herself.

"Not! This! Time!"

Elaine charged her, and the two fell to the ground again. Shanice scrambled to lock her arm around Elaine's neck, forcing her into a headlock and cutting off her circulation.

Wham!

Elaine jabbed her elbow into Shanice's broken ribs.

She moaned aloud in pain for the first time.

Wham. The second blow loosened her hold slightly.

Just hold on, Gib.

Wham. The third blow made her release the grip to cover her ribs.

Elaine stood to her feet and lifted Shanice to hers. "I was always better than you, Gibson," she said as she pushed Shanice as hard as she could.

Overboard.

Splash.

Shanice's body hit the water and sank out of sight.

20

BRAVO FIGHTS

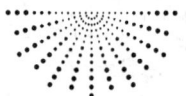

*S*plash.

The roar of the waves swallowed up any signs of life.

Elaine and the doctor walked over to the mini-boat they'd towed with them and climbed off The Defiant, heading back to shore.

The doctor began to tremble and sob openly.

"What's wrong, Dr. Packard?"

"You can't just keep killing people, Elaine."

"I don't know what you mean, Doctor."

"You just pushed that woman overboard."

"Now, how can that be when we were never here?"

"What are you talking about? We're here right n—"

"We were never here, Doctor. We prepped for the storm tonight."

"Oh my God. First Jackson, and now Gibson. She was right, you are crazy."

Elaine stepped away from the controls of the boat. "How could I have possibly killed Jackson? I wasn't even in the building when he died."

"Oh, please Elaine, I saw his file. He needed a medical discharge and intensive rehabilitation from PTSD, and you just kept pushing him past his limits."

"I freed Jackson from a lifetime of pain and prescription drugs. He was a ticking time-bomb, and no one was going to stop him."

"And you pulled the pin on that bomb and made sure Sergeant Winters was there to watch it go off."

Elaine rolled her eyes dismissively. "A necessary causality in war. Why not let his death help someone else? Look how it turned out. Marcus needed that little nudge to become the man he is today. If Jackson didn't die, Brothers in Arms would never have been born. Marcus needed that push."

"You were his therapist! He trusted you with his innermost thoughts to save his life, and instead of helping him, you pushed him over the edge."

"Oh, please, save the morality lecture. We all signed up and pledged our lives to die for other men's causes. Jackson forfeited his life the moment he enlisted in the U.S. Army."

"For his country, Elaine! Not so you could live out your warped little wet dreams."

"What I did was for the good of the country! Marcus Winters is an outstanding leader, and a great man. Do you know how many soldier's lives he saved overseas? How many he's helped in the last few months alone with this program? He is one of the best things to ever happen to the U.S. military, so if a couple of soldiers have to die for that cause, I can live with the collateral damage."

"Holt, I'm not an idiot. You didn't do this for your country, you did it for yourself. I've stayed silent long enough. I... I can't do this anymore."

"And what is that supposed to mean?"

"It means I'm done. I won't tell anyone about tonight. But I'm not writing any more prescriptions, or providing any more medication so you can drug Sergeant Winters."

Elaine raised her eyebrows, started by the statement. "We all have a role to play, Doctor, and yours is far from over."

"What more do you want from me? I just said I won't tell anyone what you did, but I can no longer be a part of this. I'm not prescribing drugs to fake a condition we both know he's not suffering from. I'm not going to jail for you, Elaine—"

Elaine grabbed the man by his green poncho and seethed, "You will do what I tell you to do, when I tell you! Unless you want the contents of your personal hard drive leaked online. I wonder, how do you think the unstable soldiers like Jackson will respond when they find out what you did to those innocent boys and girls when you were in pediatrics? You think prison is the worst of your worries? Believe me, prison would be a vacation from what's in store for you if I point any of these loose cannons in your direction."

Elaine watched as beads of sweat formed below Dr. Packard's receding hairline.

"Y—you wouldn't do that, because you have too much to lose. I'll tell them the truth about how you were behind Jackson's death, and what you did to Sergeant Gibson and what you're doing to Sergeant Winters. I know secrets, too."

Elaine smirked at the doctor and released him. She sat back at the helm of the boat.

"Well, it would be your word against mine, Doctor. And if I'm honest, I like my odds there. After all, like you just said, you wrote all the prescriptions for Marcus, and you were the last person seen alive with Gibson. Not to mention Jackson's death was well-documented as a suicide with the MP's and my own professional notes.

"I, on the other hand, have physical evidence of your crimes. I don't think you'll like how that will end. Riddle me this, Doctor, how long do you think it will take for a base full of trained killers to ask if you did something to one of their children? Men trained in abduction and torture to get the answers they want. You think Gibson is tough? These guys will keep you alive just to make you look forward to the day they end your miserable life."

She leaned in and put her hand on his shoulder. "But even in the best-case scenario, let's say it all goes your way. What do you think the outcome will be?"

The doctor shook nervously while Elaine continued.

"I need you to put that big brain of yours to work, Dr. Packard. If I go to jail, you're going to be right there alongside me, because I'll make a deal. They'll trust a pretty girl like me, and yes, they may have me on the hook for the drugs, but what do you think they'll do to you?

"Jail doesn't scare me, Dr. Packard. I'm a combat veteran in the best shape of my life, in my physical prime. But it should terrify an out-of-shape, 58-year-old pedophile."

Dr. Packard openly sobbed. "That was a long time ago and I am not the same person anymore."

"Dr. Packard, there's no statute of limitations for child molestation. At least that's what I've been telling my patients who are victims of the crime. And believe me, Doctor, some of the details they share with me about what would happen if they got their hands on an offender… Well, there's no good way to say it, because it's just downright gruesome."

Elaine watched Dr. Packard process the weight of her words. She walked over to him and gently put her hand on his shoulder. "But of course, if all of this stays between us, these horrible events will never come to pass. If we just stick to the plan. So, it's your choice, Doc. Choose wisely."

As they docked the boat, the pair headed to her car. Elaine drove as the doctor mulled over his options in silence.

She parked at the edge of the base, turned off the headlights and turned to Packard.

"Do we have an und—"

"We're clear, Elaine. Just let me out of here."

Elaine unlocked the car door. "Go through this clearing and it will take you back to the base. The less we're seen together today, the better."

The doctor got out of the car and began to move through the rain and over the torn fence back onto base.

Elaine restored her headlights and drove home.

She pondered the events of the night, ensuring she had covered all her bases. When she arrived home, she noticed her hand was bleeding, no doubt from the fight with Shanice.

"Gotta clean the car tomorrow," she mused aloud.

She made quick work of bandaging her hand with the first aid kit she kept in the backseat. She had reached her condo door and inserted the key when she heard a voice behind her.

"Elaine."

Her heart sunk as she turned around. "M—Marcus! What—Are….? You scared me half to death. What are you doing here?"

"I wanted to talk. I would've used the key you gave me a while ago, but under the circumstances, I felt it was inappropriate. Where are you coming from? It's late. Is your hair wet?"

"I… I went for a drive and got caught in the storm. What are you doing here? What do you want?"

"Can I come inside?"

"I… um, look, I'm exhausted. I think it's best to do this tomorrow."

She wanted to talk, but wasn't sure if she was totally prepared for any discussions just yet.

She needed to make sure she got rid of her bag, and any other evidence to cover her tracks once Gibson's body showed up. Marcus had to leave.

She opened the door to walk in when he persisted. "Listen, what I have to say won't take long, but it's important."

She didn't have time for this, but she couldn't leave him out in the rain. "Fine, come in," she said reluctantly.

She could tell her reaction surprised him. Still, the quicker he could leave, the sooner she could finish cleaning up after today's events.

As she walked through the door and placed her keys on the table, Marcus walked into the living room.

"What happened to your hand?" he asked, noticing the blood seeping through the bandage.

Elaine panicked slightly and replied defensively. "I… cut myself earlier. You said it would be quick? I have an early start tomorrow."

"Right." He nodded as he walked closer to her.

As his lover and therapist, she'd trained herself on every inflection of his voice and facial expression, yet for the first time, she couldn't tell what was on his mind. She'd never seen this look in his eyes before. There was only one thing she could think of.

Does he know? How could he know? You're so stupid, Elaine. Stupid, stupid, stupid!

Her mind was racing. She wasn't sure if he was here to kill her, or if he'd call the police. She wasn't sure why he was there. He had to have followed her.

You have to run. Shoot him!

But I love him. I could never hurt him.

Shoot him in the arm. It will give you time to escape. You're so stupid. How did you get caught?

As her inner dialogue argued with itself, her hands trembled.

Something Marcus noticed. "You're shivering, where did you—"

"What do you want, Marcus? Why are you here? Like I said, I've had a busy day and I'm tired. If this can wait until the mor—"

"I thought about what you said. And you're right, I've always put you second. When Gibson came back, I was just happy to have my old second-in-command around. Maybe we both were exploring where we were in our lives, but… there's no spark there. She's always going to be a good friend, but just that."

"You came all this way to tell me that? I appreciate it. Now, if you'll excuse me, I—"

"And then there's Kendra. I won't deny I love Kendra, and a part of me always will. But when I think about the sum of my life, the last six months have been the happiest I've ever been, and that's in large part due to you."

The words stopped her in her tracks. Suddenly Gibson's death, the doctor's cowardness… none of it mattered.

She looked at him with large, hopeful eyes. "It… it is?"

"Elaine, I've never been with someone who has worked so hard to make me happy, and it's well past time I stopped taking that for granted."

The words startled her.

Still, her task was simple: she had a long, unplanned night ahead, and she needed to make sure there was nothing linking her to what she'd just done.

"Marcus, I appreciate what you're saying, but I've—"

"Listen, Elaine. When I found out about my diagnosis, you were right there. And you've stayed by my side. You've been by my side for better or worse, until death. What I'm trying to say is, it would be a great honor if you were my wife, until… the end."

Elaine took a deep breath. It was the one thing she'd been waiting to hear since the day he'd saved her life. It was all she'd ever wanted.

Just minutes ago, she'd been begging him to leave. She needed to retrace her steps and make sure there were no loose ends, but none of that mattered now. She couldn't risk him changing his mind.

Her eyes softened. Everything she'd been through, killing Gibson and Jackson, was worth it for this feeling.

"Marcus, I'm very fragile. Please don't toy with my emotions today. I don't think I could take it."

She dropped her purse as Marcus got to one knee and pulled out a princess-cut diamond ring.

"I didn't come to play. It's time I start acting like the man you see me as. Will you marry me, Elaine Holt?"

Her heart fluttered. Her wildest dream was coming true.

"Yes, I will marry you. I will become Mrs. Sergeant Marcus Winters."

She squealed in excitement as he stood.

As she held him, she cried tears of joy. She looked up at him. "I promise you, as long as we're together, I'll do everything in my power to make you happy. We'll fight together to make sure you live as long as possible."

2 1

K.I.A

6 *months later*
"Babe, hurry! You're gonna be late," Elaine called as she looked at the two paint options for the room she was examining. After a spell, she chose ice blue, and dipped the paintbrush in the paint. It wasn't long before Marcus walked in and hugged her from behind, kissing her on the neck.

"Elaine, what are you doing?"

"I'm just getting a head-start on the nursery."

"But you're not pregnant."

"Yet. I'm not pregnant *yet*."

Marcus leaned in and kissed her, taking the paintbrush out of her hands. "Babe, you know I love you, but this is exactly why people think you're crazy."

Elaine turned around and kissed him passionately. "Luckily for me, I don't care what people think. I only care what you and that wonderful soldier you have in your pants thinks. And I can't wait until he gives me a little soldier of my own to carry.

"Now, with your permission, Sergeant, I'd like to get back to painting our future captain's nursery room. Besides, with all the kinky

123

stuff we've done in here, I think a fresh coat of paint is necessary, don't you think?"

Marcus laughed. "I mean, if what you're manifesting comes true, we're just gonna be doing more nasty stuff in this room, and everywhere else. But if it makes you happy, do it."

"Thank you, babe. I'm glad you're starting to see things my way, Sergeant Winters," she said with a wink.

"Happy wife, happy life, right?" he said, slapping her ass cheeks.

He pulled her in close when she stopped him.

"Babe, we can't right now."

"Sure we can, I just nee—"

"No, I'm serious, Marcus. Last time we started up in this room, I missed the IVF appointment, and I can't miss another one because the penalty is crazy expensive."

Marcus released her. "Babe, it's not like we don't have the money. With these government contracts continuing to roll in the way they are, we can pay for IVF, adopt a kid, *and* pay for a nanny to watch them both. I am sorry I'll miss your appointment, though"

"Are you excited about your trip to Houston?"

Marcus paused in his tracks. He grabbed Elaine's hands and whispered, "Babe, listen, I know you're probably uncomfortable with me going down to Houston alone, and that's why I want you to come with me. Besides, the way I'm feeling now, I don't think you're gonna need IVF to get pregnant."

"Marcus, stop it, you nasty man," Elaine said playfully as she pushed his hand away.

She looked at him and kissed him on the lips softly. "I'm not worried about you going to Houston, babe. I know you love me."

"Then come early and stay with me, please."

"Babe, I still have work and—"

"I don't know if I can be down there that long without you. Besides, the new meds have me feeling great, but—"

"You don't want to have any more episodes."

"It's like you're my good-luck charm, you know. Ever since I met you,

my life has gotten better, and getting married to you was the best decision I've ever made. My business is thriving. We have twelve Army bases
on contract and you've been there to help me open every single one."

"Okay, Marcus. I'll come down as soon as I'm done with my
appointment, okay? I want you to have a good time with Hayes. You
boys could use a couple of days alone…. but only a couple."

"Yeah. You know Hayes, after a while, he's gonna get on my damn
nerves with one of his conspiracy theories."

"Well, I tell you what, if you can find a way to meet me in the
airport parking lot before you leave, I'll give you a BJ."

Marcus grinned and kissed her. "Consider it done." He squeezed
her ass before trotting out of the room.

Elaine smiled with the bliss of a schoolgirl. She put down the
paintbrush and walked into the living room as Marcus was searching
for a few last things for the trip.

"Your socks are in the bag already, and your wallet is on the
microwave, and Uber Eats should be here any minute now with those
catfish nuggets you like from Momma J's."

Marcus smiled empathetically. "You're pretty damn good to me,
you know that?"

"You just wait till I get down to Houston with you. I've got a pair
of cowboy boots and a ten-gallon hat I'm gonna wear. I'm determined
to win the bucking bronco contest." She rubbed her hand across the
crotch of her husband.

He leaned in and kissed her and then pushed her hand away. "Can
I just point out that while most men complain about their sex lives
after marriage, ours somehow went up a notch?"

"Baby, you have given me everything I've ever wanted in life. All I
want to do is spend the rest of my life thanking you for making me so
happy. As long as I'm around, you'll never have to jack your dick
again."

"I'll see you at the airport."

"I can't wait. Say, before you leave, what's the weather like down
there this time of year?"

"Hot as shit. Doesn't matter what time of year you're asking, that's the answer. Can you believe Brothers in Arms is growing like this?"

"Of course I can. You were born to do great things, Sergeant Winters. It's time they pay you properly for your services."

"No shit. Being a military contractor is where it's at. It's crazy, because this morning I saw on the news that the guy who got shot by the cops down there is out of his coma."

Elaine leaned into him. "Lucas, something, right?"

"Kimble. Lucas Kimble."

"It's not the first time you've mentioned this. Why is it a sore spot for you?"

Marcus put his wallet in his jeans and said, "It's just… He's been sleeping for a year, and I've been fighting for my life for the same amount of time. When I first heard it on the news, I wondered if I'd live to see if he'd ever wake up. Now he's awake and I'm—"

"You're thriving."

"I am thriving. Still on my meds, but taking it each day. Thanks to you."

Marcus kissed her on the cheek as the doorbell rang.

He opened the door to Ryan wearing a Houston Astros baseball cap and a blue fitted T-shirt with stonewashed blue jeans. He held a package in his hands.

"Is that my food?"

"Hell, it's someone's. These nuggets are pretty damn good. Is this catfish?"

Marcus snatched the bag out of his friend's hands and walked back into the living room.

"Ready to roll?" Marcus asked as he ate what was left of his food.

"Yeah, I'm all packed up, brother. I want to get to the airport and sit in that room with those guys with the big bucks and drink a few cocktails before we get on the plane."

"The Admiral's quarters."

"Whatever. All I know is I get to be hammered sitting in first class. Is Psycho Barbie coming with us or not?"

"Hayes!"

"My bad, brother. Still getting used to this weird shit," Ryan said as Elaine interjected, "It's okay. I've grown used to Ryan's surly attitude. You boys go have fun. Marcus, don't forget."

"I won't. Love you."

"That was gross," Ryan said as the pair walked out of the door.

They got to the sidewalk when they were met by General Reese.

Surprised by his visit, Marcus asked. "General? You came to see us off to Houston?"

"I didn't, but I am glad I caught you. Is now a bad time?"

"General!" Elaine said as she walked out to join the trio.

The General nodded. "Actually, what I have to say involves the both of you."

"What's going on?" Marcus asked, curious about the ominous tone General Reese had taken.

The general took off his hat, rubbed his eyes and took a deep breath. After a spell, he said. "About thirty-six hours ago, the FBI conducted a sting and found Dr. Packard trying to lure a young child into his home. When they apprehended him, they found some... disturbing stuff."

"Oh, my God, what is it?"

"Kids, Winters... he's into kids. He's in custody, and he's not willing to say anything until he talks to his therapist, who, according to him, is Elaine Holt-Winters.

THE SAGA CONTINUES in *Seduction II*

M.I.A

$\mathcal{M}$ ay we sow "The storm may be over, but its impact lives on. Prolonged coastal flooding, beach erosion, strong winds, high surf, rip currents and heavy rains will continue to encompass a much larger area of the Southeast."

Click.

The man in a red flannel jacket turned off his radio and walked to the front of his log cabin. He assessed the debris and nodded, walking back into his home.

"Coffee smells done," he said aloud and walked over to the kitchen to pour himself a cup. It was hot to taste. He held his lip, now slightly singed by the heat of the java.

He walked to his living room and sat down to open his crossword puzzle.

"They have thirty-six black keys," he pondered aloud as he scanned for the proper place to put the answer to the question.

"P-I-A-N—"

Woof, woof.

The man put his crossword puzzle down and picked up his 9 mm Beretta. He walked towards the back of the room.

He tapped the door and glanced in the bedroom, his dog barking at the woman in the bedroom. He ordered the dog out of the room and stored away the pistol in the small of his back.

"Good, you're awake. I was getting worried about you."

"Where am I?"

"First things first, how do you feel?"

"I feel like... I should be dead."

"I would have to agree with you there. Tell me, what's the last thing you remember."

"I was... in a storm. That's all..." The woman started hyperventilating.

The man reached for a glass of water and handed it to the woman, who took the bottle and finished it quickly, calming herself.

The man leaned over her. "Take your time. It'll come to you."

"Why am I handcuffed?" the woman asked, realizing one of her hands was chained to the bedpost.

The man raised both of his hands calmly. "Lady, I don't know you, and I'm not big on letting strangers in my home, but it was either that or watch you die. So, it's as much for my safety as it is yours. Now tell me, do you remember your name?"

The woman nervously rubbed her free hand across her necklace. As she touched her dog tags, she closed her eyes.

"Gibson. My name is Shanice Gibson."

SHANICE'S STORY continues in
Gibson: A Money, Power & Sex Short
available in one week.

ABOUT THE AUTHOR

Norian Love is a best-selling author, screen-writer, songwriter, and poet, whose character-rich storytelling and creative world-building is swiftly setting him apart as one of the top writers in the black romance genre. His latest release, Autumn: A Love Story, was the recipient of the Association of Black Romance Writers 2021 Book of the Year Award. Autumn's complementary poetic journal, Blue: Love Letters to Fatima, also became a number one best-seller, giving him the unique distinction of having number one releases across multiple genres. He was a finalist for the 2021 Black Authors Rock, Author of the Year Award, as well as a finalist for the 2022 Romance Slam Jam Best Erotic Romance EMMA Award. He is working on completing the highly anticipated Money, Power, & Sex series and is currently serving as the head screenwriter for the University of Houston HIV Awareness campaign.

Penning the hashtag, #blacklovematters, Norian has been garnering accolades for his work from his reviewers, fans, peers, book clubs, and several podcasts. His books are sold worldwide and are published in print, eBook, and audio formats.

To learn more, visit www.norianlove.com or follow him across most social media outlets at @norianlove.